Lone Star Reunion

Lone Star Reunion

A Texas Justice Romance

Justine Davis

Lone Star Reunion
Copyright© 2020 Justine Davis
Tule Publishing First Printing, February 2020

The Tule Publishing, Inc.

ALL RIGHTS RESERVED

First Publication by Tule Publishing 2020

Cover design by The Killion Group

No part of this book may be used or reproduced in any manner whatsoever without written permission except in the case of brief quotations embodied in critical articles and reviews.

This is a work of fiction. Names, characters, places, and incidents are products of the author's imagination or are used fictitiously. Any resemblance to actual events, locales, organizations, or persons, living or dead, is entirely coincidental.

ISBN: 978-1-951786-38-0

Chapter One

"THINK HE'LL COME back?"

"No idea. Not sure I would."

"Wouldn't blame him. I know a little about how it feels to be the one who's different."

Sage Highwater heard her brothers talking from where she stood in the back entry, pulling off her boots. While the Highwater ranch house was a place with floors intended to tolerate all the effects of ranch work, her boots were particularly muddy today; giving a horse a bath tended to have that result.

She had no idea what or who they were talking about, but Sean's comment about being different didn't give her the qualms it once had. Not anymore. Not since Elena had turned his life around simply by falling in love with him.

She was smiling to herself about that, and about how well Poke, their prime reining prospect, had done in their training session today. She was going to have to seriously consider whether to ease off on the intensive training. She didn't want the sweet, agile dun to go sour before the big competition this summer in Oklahoma City. He was—

"Does she know yet?"

Slater again, interrupting her thoughts with that unspecific "she." Once not so very long ago, she herself would have been the only one that could have referred to, here in this house, spoken in that manner. But now it could be Shane's Lily, Slater's Joey, or Sean's Elena. And while that made her feel a slight pang at how quickly everything was changing, her delight in all her brothers' happiness quickly erased it.

"Does which *she* know what?" she asked as she came into the kitchen where Shane and Slater were leaning against the kitchen island and Sean was sitting on one of the stools beside it, his boot heels hooked over the top rung so he could rest his elbows on his knees.

All three men winced and went still, which answered her question. She flipped the long, dark braid that had fallen forward as she'd shed her boots back over her shoulder. She abandoned her intention to head for the coffee they were all drinking and stopped, facing them and crossing her arms.

"Well?" she demanded.

Slater and Sean looked at Shane. Her eldest brother sighed. Did he ever get tired, truly tired, of being the father substitute of the Highwaters? He was so good at it, and had been ever since he'd been forced to step into those huge, paternal boots at twenty-two, that she didn't often wonder how much he minded the role he'd never had the option to turn down.

Her tall, strong brother, who wore the badge of Last Stand police chief as easily as he wore the dark gray Resistol cowboy hat that was part of his daily unofficial uniform, set down his coffee mug. And when he spoke it was in the blunt, no-nonsense tones of his job. For which Sage was glad, considering what he said.

"Peter Parrish drove his car into Buchanan Lake last night. He didn't get out."

Sage was proud that she barely twitched, not even inwardly, at the name. "Drunk again, I suppose?" That came out nice and even, she thought.

"Tests aren't back yet, but it looks likely."

The irony bit deep. "Nice way to throw away a lot of sacrifice," she said, and that didn't come out so calmly.

They were all silent then. Watching her. And the first words she'd heard, from Slater, played back in her head.

Think he'll come back?

A shivery chill swept over her.

Scott.

They were talking about Scott.

There would be a funeral, and of course both brothers would be expected. Robbie, the treasured one, who had been part of that unbreakable, impenetrable unit of four…and the useless one, the misfire, the one who had been nothing but trouble and treated as such. The one they'd tried to give away when he couldn't fulfill the purpose he'd been conceived for.

Scott.

The boy who had been the proverbial black sheep of a family already dealt a harsh blow.

The boy who had been the talk of Last Stand, and not in a good way.

The boy who had finally escaped the weight of both his

reputation and his family.

The boy she had loved but who had, without a word, left her behind to do it.

THE MOMENT SCOTT Parrish got out of the rental car he knew he'd made a mistake.

And why are you surprised? Just because you managed to stop making them—most of the time—elsewhere?

He had the crazy thought that maybe it was this place, that there was something in the air of Last Stand, Texas, that made him lose his gyroscope. Or maybe it was simply the proximity to the only people left in the world who could still make him angry. Which was a hell of a thought, given where he'd been and what he'd done in the last ten years.

He shifted the large camouflage duffel bag on his shoulder. It wasn't really heavy. He hadn't brought much, because he wasn't going to be here that long. Thank God. He'd be out of this place he hated with more heat than a Middle Eastern desert by Sunday. Even that was longer than he wanted to be here, but it would give him long enough to finish the two tasks he'd set himself. One because he owed it, the other because his brother, the innocent, blameless one, the one he'd once tried so hard to help, had begged him.

You've got to come, Scott.
Why? He didn't give a damn about me when he was alive.
He did!
He didn't.

He'd left it at that, because he didn't want to hurt the brother who had already had so much taken from him. Figuratively and literally. They'd never been close, he and Robbie, because they'd never had the chance. In the beginning, when he'd first been old enough to understand he'd tried, so often, to help, but had been slapped down so hard he'd quickly learned his help wasn't needed or wanted. And always between them was the other brother whose funeral he was here for, the one who had had so many sacrifices made for him, but had thrown them all away by getting behind the wheel drunk.

The rebellious thought hit that if he was going to die anyway, maybe it would have been better if that pernicious blood cancer had taken him when he'd first been diagnosed.

And now you're wishing death on a four-year-old? Way to give them more reason to hate you, Parrish.

He took in a deep breath and looked around. Maybe it was fitting that now, when he was at complete loose ends, he was back here in the place where his life had hit its lowest point. He wondered rather idly if it was a sign that he really had gotten past those grim days that he was able to look at the current state of his life, which most people would probably be distressed over, and think merely that he needed a little time to figure out what he was going to do.

After ten years of having to make split-second, life-changing—or life-ending—decisions, this was nothing.

He walked to the back of the rental car to stow the duffel in the trunk. A marked Last Stand police unit cruised by, slowly. He didn't recognize the officer at the wheel. Which had to mean she'd been here less than ten years, because he guessed just about every cop in town had caught him at something, one time or other. Sometimes it amazed him, what he'd gotten away with without ending up locked up.

Because they all felt sorry for your family.

The curse of small towns. Everybody knew everything about everyone. And if they didn't, Mr. Diaz saw to it that they soon did. Scott guessed the crusty old man probably still ran the feed store with an iron fist, maybe the city council too, in addition to his unofficial job of being the nexus of the Last Stand grapevine.

Scott unzipped the bag, grabbed the large, heavy manila envelope, then rezipped it. He slammed the trunk shut and glanced at the departing police car once more. And finally, as he'd known he would have to, let in the thought he'd been dodging.

Sage.

The one person in Last Stand who had understood, who had been sad with him and for him, had been angry on his behalf. And he'd had to leave without seeing her. They'd made it clear any screwup between his hearing with the judge and when he left town voided the deal. And if there was anyone who could tempt him into screwing up it was Sage Highwater. And so he hadn't dared to see her one last time, had resorted to the worst cop-out, leaving her a note.

It hadn't been only that he'd been terrified any extra minute that passed might snatch this chance away from him, it was that he hadn't dared risk the wrath of her protective big brother, the very cop who had caught him that last time. Not to mention her other two big brothers. Nobody messed with the Highwaters, and when it came to protecting their little sister, they were a united front.

Not that he blamed them. He'd been far too much trouble, and not nearly good enough for the likes of Sage Highwater. He'd known that even then. It was the only thing that had enabled him to resist her. Even at sixteen she'd been beautiful, in that wild, boundless Texas girl way, with her long, dark hair and bluebonnet blue eyes.

And she'd wanted him. For God knows what insane reason, she'd wanted him and had made it clear. He'd never felt anything quite so heady, before or since.

You're just lucky she wasn't the cop in that car.

He had no doubts she'd achieved her goal of wearing the Last Stand uniform. Because Sage with her mind set was a near-irresistible force. And who knew that better than him?

His jaw clenched, and determined, he shoved the memories back into their cage and focused on what he had to do. He'd become very good at that in the ten years since he'd left this place. And he wasn't going to let coming back to Last Stand—temporarily—change that.

Chapter Two

"Thank you for seeing me, Your Honor."

"We're not in a courtroom now—I think simply Judge will do. Sit down."

"Judge, then."

Scott sat as ordered, glancing around the room. It hadn't changed much in ten years, this place called the judge's chambers. He remembered it, albeit a little vaguely. Various framed certificates on one wall, photographs on another, not of the judge himself but others who clearly had significance to him, although Scott had no idea why, since he hadn't recognized them.

Except one, sort of. He'd realized later—he'd been too scared when he'd been sitting here—the reason the man in the top right photo, in a police uniform with stars on the collar, looked familiar. Because he had the look of a Highwater. Dark hair, bright blue eyes, the steady gaze. And he'd figured out it had to be Last Stand Police Chief Steven Highwater. Sage's father. Mowed down on the street not far from here, when she'd been only fourteen. Some said he'd been pushed in front of that truck, but Scott knew Sage staunchly refused to believe it. Of course that was then.

Maybe she'd changed her mind.

But there were two people he recognized up there now. Because there was a new one, toward the center. A man with the same look, in the same uniform. A man Scott had spent some time with, although there had been stripes on his sleeve, not stars on his collar at the time. Shane Highwater.

"My condolences on your brother," Judge Morales said. Scott stifled a grimace and said nothing. For a silent moment Judge Morales simply looked at him. Then, quietly, he said, "It must seem like such a waste. After everything your family went through."

"And then he throws it away?" The words burst out as if they'd been under pressure. As they had been; the pressure of his not wanting to show it had gotten to him. He was past that. Way past. Or so he'd thought.

"Exactly," the judge said.

But Scott was not about to drag out old, tattered, dirty laundry, not here, not in front of this man who had seen…something in him, when he himself hadn't been able to see anything but pain and anger. He was going to say what he had to say, pay what little he could on a debt too large to ever repay to this man, then do his duty to a family who'd never wanted him in the first place, and then get out of this town.

He took a deep breath. "I know this is ten years late, but I wanted to thank you."

He knew he sounded stiff, but he couldn't help it. Not much intimidated him anymore, but this man still did. Even without the judge's robes, there was something about his air of authority that reminded him of other men with bars or stars on their collars. The men who had helped mold him into the man he was now. Odd though; the judge had seemed older ten years ago. Obviously it must have been his own blind youth at the time, but now he didn't look much older than the elder Chief Highwater in that photograph, and he knew the chief had been killed at forty-three. Maybe it had been that air of gravity the judge had had at the time.

His mind seemed to slip back to that day, when he'd sat here before, scared but defiant, certain he was going to end up in jail but not certain he wouldn't be better off. Wondering if maybe he belonged there.

Have you ever struck someone in anger?
Yes, sir. Once.
Who.
My younger brother.
Why?

He'd blinked at that. No one had ever cared why. But the judge had just waited for an answer.

He never stood up for himself. He just let them use him. I was trying to wake him up.
Did it work?
No, sir.
Did you ever do it again?
No, sir.
Do you drink? Use drugs?

He'd pondered that one for a split second. Decided not to lie. *Yes and no.*

Get drunk?

Just buzzed. Sometimes he had just needed that buzz, to drown out the anger. He'd wondered, back then, if his father even noticed the missing beers. Wondered if maybe he preferred Scott buzzed, because at least then he wasn't in his face.

Ever steal anything worth over a hundred dollars?

No, sir. Only because Sergeant Highwater caught me this time before I could, he'd thought. And then, with said sergeant's admonition to be honest in mind, he added, *But I almost did.*

What's the worst thing you actually have done?

Besides hit my brother? I...trespassed. A lot.

Where?

A place down on the creek.

Where?

Down at the big bend.

The Buckley place?

I wasn't looking to steal anything! I'm not that stupid, to steal from a Ranger.

Then it should be no problem to answer.

Yes. Only when it was hot. I wanted to cool off in the creek and that's the best spot.

Take any friends with you?

No. Not strictly speaking. The only one he'd call a friend met him there.

No hanging out with all your buddies, plotting mayhem?

Don't have any.

He'd meant it. Anyone willing to put up with his moods had long since fallen away by the time he'd turned seventeen.

And, he'd thought rather belligerently then, even if he had, he wouldn't rat them out anyway. It had taken him a while to realize that had been the judge's way of finding out exactly how alienated he really was.

The long silence suddenly registered and he snapped out of the reverie, wondering how long he'd been lost in that memory. The judge was just looking at him, in that same assessing way he had back then.

He made himself focus, and went on. "You didn't write me off, despite my...insistence on getting in trouble. Instead of sending me to juvie, you gave me the chance to make something of myself. I just wanted you to know I didn't waste it." *Unlike my brother, who wasted it all.*

He laid the folder on the man's desk. His military record, replete with his training progress, his deployment and mission records, and a list of commendations, awards, and medals that while not overly distinguished was certainly more than respectable.

Judge Morales scanned the file, then leaned back in his chair. "I can see that you didn't waste it. But then, I already knew."

"Kept tabs on me?" Scott wasn't surprised. The man took his responsibilities beyond seriously.

"Only until I was certain Shane Highwater's assessment of you was correct."

He blinked. Sage's brother? The one who had warned him off his little sister—well, to be fair, all the Highwater men had—had done...what? "Sergeant Highwater?" he said, rather blankly.

"Chief, now."

"Yeah. I heard. Not surprised. But back then...he talked to you?"

Judge Morales smiled. "Why do you think I agreed to the hearing, and interceded with the recruiters? And why do you think Ken Herdmann agreed not to press charges? Shane talked him out of it."

Scott swallowed, remembering. He'd spent that night at the police station, to his surprise not locked up in a cell but in the watch commander's office, which was apparently the position then Sergeant Highwater was occupying that night. And they had talked. At least, the sergeant had talked, although eventually he'd gotten to the point where he would at least nod or shake his head in response.

"He pleaded your case rather intensely. Told me none of it was your fault, really, which I found fascinating given what I knew of him not being one to lightly excuse blatant infractions. He said you just needed to escape an impossible situation, and to have a goal, a path to follow, a path that would lead to feeling valued. That if you had that, you'd do well."

An image popped into Scott's mind, of the tall, blue-eyed man in uniform finding him that night, in the moment he'd been about to try hot-wiring the editor of *The Defender*'s classic Mustang. Given he thought the guy hated him, he'd been stunned at the man's kindness.

The judge smiled then. "Normally I would question that confident assessment from a man as young as the sergeant was. But this was a man who had stepped into his father's shoes more than admirably for his own family, essentially finishing the raising of his younger siblings, and so I trusted his instincts."

Scott stared at the judge, completely blindsided. He'd be the first to admit he hadn't been totally aware of what was going on back then. All he'd been sure of at seventeen was that he'd finally gone that step too far, and done something that would land him in jail, not just in a holding cell awaiting his stiff-lipped mother or enraged father. It didn't matter which, really, either one would be furious at being dragged from Pete's side, at being torn from that alliance of four, especially by the one who didn't belong.

The one they'd tried to get rid of, once they'd determined he could not serve their purpose. He remembered he'd even wondered if they'd show up at all. Maybe they'd just leave him to rot, like an overripe apple they'd bought by mistake.

When he'd eventually wound up in these very chambers, he'd expected the worst. Instead he'd been given a chance. And he'd grabbed at it without thinking much about it, and when he realized an hour or two later it meant he would really be shed of the Parrish family drama, he'd felt a sense of liberation he'd never known before.

"I had the feeling he was sensitive to your plight because of his own brother," the judge was saying now, and Scott snapped back to the present as the words confirmed his earlier thought.

"Kane?" The judge nodded. "He never turned up?"

"Not yet. But they are still searching."

He drew back slightly. "It's been…what, twelve years?"

"The Highwaters do not give up easily. As Shane Highwater did not give up on you. I'm very glad you've proven him right." He leaned forward and closed the file, but his gaze was fixed on Scott. "I appreciate the thanks. Not many bother."

"I owed it to you."

"That you feel that way validates my decision ten years ago. And will probably encourage me to give some other kid a chance, should the occasion arise. So that's to your credit, too."

That was something that had never occurred to Scott, that him making good could somehow help some other desperate kid down the line. It made him feel unexpectedly gratified.

"But," the judge said, "I think there's someone else you need to thank more than me."

"I…guess so."

With a warm smile, Judge Morales picked up the file and handed it back to him. "Show him this. It says all that needs to be said."

Chapter Three

SAGE HIGHWATER YAWNED and stretched as she waited for the coffee to finish dripping. It had been a long night, but when her neighbor and best friend, Jessie McBride, had sent up an SOS she'd never hesitated. Jessie's left leg had been badly broken in an accident last month, and Sage had willingly been on call ever since. And last night one of Jessie's rescue mustangs had been foaling.

Sage knew Jessie hated asking for help, but there was no way she could manage alone if something went wrong. So Sage had dressed hastily, pulled her long hair back in a knot to keep it out of the way, yanked on her worn boots, and run to the barn. She'd bridled Poke and leapt aboard bareback. Some would criticize her using their prized reining prospect for something like this, but Sage figured the better he adapted to unexpected things outside the arena, the less he'd get rattled by them inside the arena.

Once through the fence that delineated the Highwater ranch from the McBrides' it had been an exhilarating mad dash through the moonlight. It turned out the competent mare delivered smoothly, and soon there was a long-legged little filly nursing from her exhausted but already devoted mother. And Sage counted the loss of sleep a small price to pay for the lovely sight.

She could have done without the discussion they'd had as they waited to see if the mare needed any help, though. It was Jessie who'd brought up the subject of Scott.

"Maybe he won't come," she'd said. "I wouldn't blame him. Even my dad says his parents were a couple of the most unpleasant people he'd ever encountered, even before Pete—who was even worse—got sick."

Since Doc McBride was one of the most circumspect men she'd ever met, Sage knew what it would take to get him to say even that much. The Parrishes were apparently rude and cold to everyone outside their little clique of four, not just their middle son.

She'd staggered back into bed about the time everyone else was stirring. And now she had the house to herself. That was a rarity these days, between Shane and Lily, now engaged, Slater and Joey headed that way, and now, amazingly, Sean and Elena. The last thought made her smile, for she had known for years of her quirky, beloved brother's barely suppressed reverence for the exquisitely beautiful Elena de la Cova. And now Sage was delighted to have found the elegant, regal woman in fact had a wicked sense of humor, and more importantly, a deep, genuine love for Sean she was not afraid to declare.

Her coffee mug full now, she sat down and sipped gratefully. They'd left her a cinnamon roll—and she knew what a sacrifice that was—but she'd get to that in a minute. She yawned again, and took another swallow of coffee, willing the caffeine to hit hard and fast; she had a lot to do today.

Because it was there, she reached out and tugged the copy of the latest edition of the Last Stand newspaper, *The Defender*, to her. Lily, who freelanced for the paper, had likely brought it to the house knowing Slater was old-school and preferred the print version. And Joey championed that; as an assistant librarian she loved the feel and smell of physical books and paper. Sage had always figured it was the words that mattered, not the medium, so she'd read either way.

Idly, eyes still at half-mast as she waited for the kick, she looked at the newsprint without really seeing anything beyond the headlines. There was nothing shocking, unless you considered someone actually challenging Mr. Diaz for his seat on the city council shocking. She was sure Samuel Diaz did.

She flipped through to the last page, then idly pushed the paper away. Or started to; she stopped dead when she focused on the notice just above her fingers. She read the funeral announcement, although Lily had already told her it was this Saturday. But she refused to read the obituary, because she knew the truth behind the prettied-up facts.

She suppressed a sigh and finished pushing the paper back to where she'd found it. Felt her mind try to veer back into wondering if he really would come back for the funeral. Tried to rein it in. Why would he? He and Pete—even mentally she still refused to call him Peter as his father insisted everyone do, emphasizing that he was his namesake, his chosen one—had ever been at odds. He and his entire family had been at odds, and she knew why. Understood why, which he'd once told her no one else did.

No one else. Not any of the people who had written him off as a lost cause, the kid who dared to make trouble for a family in a battle for a life.

Sage had never written him off. Because she'd known he had good reason to be the way he was. And had wondered why no one else could see it. Why no one else could see the way he'd been tossed aside. And she wondered why no one cared that Pete Parrish Jr. was—had been—a very nasty person. She understood it was human nature to forgive just about anything in someone who had been so seriously ill, but wasn't there a line, somewhere? Did the fact that Pete had faced death as a child give him the right to become a rude, entitled, arrogant adult?

She didn't know the answer to that. Wasn't sure there was an answer to it. All she knew was that Scott had never been given a fraction of the latitude either of his brothers had. That he had paid a high, albeit different, price too. No one else seemed to understand that.

But Shane had. Or at least he had listened to her, and when the time inevitably came that he'd had to make a decision about Scott's potentially grim future, Shane had done the one thing that had given him a chance to escape.

She'd be perfectly happy, even delighted with that. If he'd bothered to say goodbye. If he'd even given her a phone call. Hell, if the man had ever seen fit to even send her a postcard.

But he never had. And every time a report appeared

about a service member killed, her heart had jammed up in her throat. It had taken her a couple of years to break herself of the habit of searching out those reports. It had been one of her vows to herself when she'd graduated high school. She would make it through the police academy, and she would quit pining after Scott Parrish. She'd accomplished the former—even if she had changed course afterward and decided to stay on the ranch—and also the latter, for the most part.

But the thought that he might come back to Last Stand for his brother's funeral nagged at her like a relentless horsefly. And she couldn't seem to make it go away.

SCOTT HADN'T PLANNED on this. He'd thought he'd see Judge Morales this morning, go to the funeral Saturday, and be gone. On to the rest of his life. He wasn't sure exactly what he was going to do with that life now, but he knew for damned sure he wasn't going to do it here.

Since he was so utterly certain—and because he needed a moment to work up to this, and now that he was out of a war zone he could take that moment—he decided to take a walk down Main Street, just to see if things had changed. It looked the same as ever, at least from here. The Catholic church still stood as it ever had, imposing and a little intimidating.

He wondered if they'd ever replaced the lock on the back gate that led to the courtyard, that old, tarnished thing that had made it so easy to sneak in. He'd spent a night or two crouched in the shadow of that wall, hiding. He wondered if Father Garza was still there, figured probably not; the priest had been ancient ten years ago.

"Feel free to come in," a cheerful voice said from his right, and he turned to see a dark-haired man in the traditional white collar carrying several bags from the hardware store, and clearly headed for the…whatever they called the rooms that were off the big one where they held mass. A much younger man than Father Garza.

"Thanks, but I'm not Catholic."

The man shrugged, and gave him a grin Father Garza never would have. "Doesn't mean you can't come in."

Scott found himself smiling back. "Thanks. I'll keep it in mind." He eyed the bags. "That's a lot of stuff."

"Painting, after which I'm sure I'll look like one of the local pinto horses. Then building some shelving. Which I'm sure will be crooked."

Scott's smile widened. He liked this guy. "Want some help lugging all that?"

"I'm good. But you could pull the door open for me."

Scott moved quickly to do so. The man stepped through and set the bags on what was obviously a worktable just inside the door. "Thank you. You can consider that your good deed for the day."

Scott grinned now. "I only have to do one?"

"All I ask from strangers. My parish, I demand a little more."

He couldn't help it, he laughed, and not solely because of

the man's unknowing play on his name. "You're a lot different from Father Garza."

"He was a very…serious man."

Scott's laugh stopped. "He's…gone?" The priest nodded. "I'm sorry."

"He made it a good long age, and went as peacefully as a man can."

Memories rose up and battered at the door of the cage Scott kept them in, of men who had died in anything but a peaceful way. "Lot to be said for that," he muttered.

"Yes." The priest held out his hand. "Christopher Nunes," he said.

Scott couldn't imagine Father Garza doing this, either. He'd always held himself a bit above. "Scott Parrish," he returned, noting that the priest's grip was strong but not declarative. And also noting that his name had registered. He grimaced inwardly, wondering just how much speculation had been going on in Last Stand about whether he'd turn up or not.

"Welcome back," was all the man said, and Scott was thankful for that. He nodded, and turned to go. He was two steps away when the priest added, "Just so you know, I fixed that back gate."

Scott whirled back. "What?"

The other man smiled, not an amused smile but one of gentle understanding. "Father Garza told me about your penchant for hiding out in the garden."

"I…he knew?"

"He did."

Scott lowered his gaze, having no idea what to say.

"He also said if he had to choose, he'd prefer you there rather than out getting into more trouble."

Scott's gaze shot back to the man's face. "But I only hid there because I knew no one would look for me there. I'm not…I wasn't…"

"One of his? That didn't matter to him, under the circumstances." The priest gave him another empathetic smile. "I've still got that old, rusty gate lock. I can put it back."

Scott managed to smile, although his mind was reeling a bit at the knowledge that he hadn't really hidden here at all. "I think I'm past that now. But thanks."

And he went on his way thinking about the things he'd never known. Father Garza knowing perfectly well he'd been, in essence, trespassing, but doing nothing. Shane Highwater going to bat for him with Mr. Herdmann and Judge Morales. Judge Morales listening, and interceding with the Marine recruiter on his behalf. He'd felt so alone back then, but apparently he hadn't been. And he wasn't sure how that made him feel.

He kept walking. Saw the Carriage House across the street, looking as it always had. Then he saw the library, and his gaze naturally shifted to the statue of Last Stand hero Asa Fuhrmann, the man who had made the run for ammunition that had allowed them to hold out just long enough, back during the revolution. It had cost him his life, but gained him a memorial everyone who lived here knew and respected.

Even him. Especially now that he knew just what it

meant to risk your life under fire.

He paused in front of the statue, and another memory hit him, this one a recent one, less than a year ago, when he'd been about to head back to the States for good.

Hey, Parrish, aren't you from a town in Texas called Last Stand?

He'd turned to look at Cindy Prentice, from the maintenance battalion that was heading out as he was heading in. *Yeah, what of it?*

That police chief there is really something.

What she had showed him was a string of videos that had been linked on a website with an embarrassing name, apparently set up by some female admirers of the man. That had been when he'd first learned that Sergeant Highwater was now the chief. He'd already seen the video of the longhorn "stampede" down this very street, the one even Highwater had laughed at. And the dash cam video of him from years ago, taking out a bomb-wearing terrorist even knowing he'd likely die doing it, was famous far beyond Last Stand, especially and approvingly in military circles.

But he hadn't known about the fiery crash last year, into this very statue where he'd again risked his own life to save the sole survivor. And when he'd gotten through all those and the Fourth of July rodeo calf-roping video that reminded him Shane Highwater was still a cowboy at heart, they'd reached the leaked video labeled "Hell or Highwater," of two clowns in a cell deciding they could take out the police chief since he must be old and weak. He'd burst out laughing. And Cindy had arched an eyebrow at him.

You know the guy, I gather?
I do. They deserved what they got.

He gave his head a sharp shake. He'd known coming back here would rattle loose a lot of memories, he just hadn't expected such a flood of them so fast. But he'd had to come, not just for the funeral. He'd only come now because of that.

He'd made the appointment to see the judge three days ago. He hadn't wanted to come so early, he'd been hoping he could see him Friday and be in and out of Last Stand in twenty-four hours, but it had been the only time available. And so he was stuck here for four days.

He'd actually been a little surprised at how easy it had been to get that appointment. He was sure the man wouldn't remember his name out of all those he'd dealt with over the years, so could just anybody walk into his chambers if they called ahead? What if it was some crazy wanting payback? But then Judge Morales was a Texas judge, and no one would be surprised if the man was more than able to take care of himself.

But as it had turned out, he had recognized Scott's name immediately. He figured it was probably thanks to Pete's name being splashed everywhere after his spectacular literal splash, driving his car into Buchanan Lake, up east of Llano. That had probably hit the judge's radar, along with everyone else's.

Crazy. As a kid he'd always figured he'd be the one to go out like that, in some drunken car crash. But the moment he'd put on the uniform he'd called a halt—even now two drinks were his limit—knowing in his gut if he didn't get through this, if he didn't pull it together, he'd blow the one chance life had thrown him.

The chance Shane Highwater had apparently thrown him.

He glanced to his right. He could see the police station from here. And up ahead, he could see the famous Last Stand Saloon, the site of that actual battle, where a pitiful number of locals—it hadn't yet become a town—had somehow held off a contingent of Santa Anna's army long enough.

He wondered who was running the place now. A Highwater uncle had been, when he'd last been here. A guy sharp enough that Scott had never even tried to bluff his way into a drink there, despite the fact he'd been tall for his age.

But now, at least, he could do it legally. *Maybe I should just go get one of those two drinks before I tackle this.*

He nearly laughed aloud at himself. Yeah, that would be good, go in and face the chief of police with booze on his breath.

He thought maybe he should call first, but he could just as easily walk the block down there and ask at the desk when the chief would be free—if he would see him at all.

Decided now, he headed that way, promising himself that drink in the saloon afterward.

He didn't really feel any qualms at stepping into the police building. It was the place where his life had started to turn around, so it was hard to feel nervous. Facing the man who was now chief was a little more daunting, but he'd left that scared, angry kid far behind him now. And he owed him.

He'd thank Shane Highwater man to man, and then he'd go to that damned funeral, somehow gut out being in the same room with his parents, remind his surviving brother there was more to life, and then he'd get the hell out of Last Stand.

For good.

Chapter Four

IT WAS SURPRISINGLY easy, in the end.
When Scott had asked about seeing the chief at the front desk, the young officer there had quickly looked to his left. Which prompted Scott to look that way as well, just in time to see the tall, dark-haired man who had been heading down a hallway pause and look back.

They made eye contact. Scott remembered those eyes from that day, and how they'd made him feel the man could see right through him, through the façade he put on to the world.

He turned back. "Scott Parrish?"

Scott was startled at the instant recognition, then realized he shouldn't be. And to his further surprise, there was no doubting the man's smile was genuine. Not the kind of smile you'd give a nuisance you'd thought yourself rid of for good. Not that he'd really expected the chief to feel that way. He figured then Sergeant Highwater had probably forgotten about him the moment he'd witnessed him signing the recruitment papers.

Scott found himself wondering how many police chiefs, even in a town as small as Last Stand, made a habit of hanging around the lobby open to the public. But he wasn't surprised this one did. He'd long known what kind of man he'd been, and clearly still was.

"Come on back to my office."

Timing, Scott thought as they walked down the hallway. If he'd gone for that drink, he'd probably be stuck waiting for an appointment. This thought made him say, "If you're busy…"

"Nothing that won't keep, for this."

The man was putting his day on hold, for him? For the scapegrace of Last Stand? What the hell had happened to this town since he'd been gone?

He glanced around the office as the chief ushered him in. It was spacious, but modestly furnished, no grand carved desks or self-importance blaring here. The only things on the walls were his commission as chief, his graduation certificate from the academy, and a photograph from both days. An American flag and the Lone Star flag flanked the credenza behind his desk chair. Which, somewhat to Scott's surprise, he didn't take. Instead he leaned against the front of the desk and smiled.

"It's good to see you," he said.

"You've come a ways," Scott said, indicating the commission.

"In a hurry," Highwater said, with a grin that somehow made the pressure ease. And he managed a smile back.

"I guess Last Stand's not comfortable without a Highwater police chief." Scott had never had a run-in with the prior Highwater chief, this man's father. But only because he hadn't worked his way up that high at that age.

The other man studied him for a moment before saying, "I'd offer my sympathy about your brother, but I'm not sure it's wanted or needed."

"It's not."

"Then never mind," was all he said, to Scott's relief. "So what can I do for you?"

"Other way around," he said. "I saw Judge Morales this morning. He told me how you really went to bat for me back then. I…didn't know. I thought you hated me."

The man frowned, then gave him a wry smile. "Because of Sage? We were all a little overprotective of her back then. She was still hurting pretty badly."

"Your father. And brother. I know."

The chief studied him for a moment. "That's what you had in common, wasn't it? Hurting, I mean."

"I think…we both understood misery."

"Yes. You did. You were adrift in hell," the chief said bluntly. "I knew if you could just get clear, you'd be all right." One corner of his mouth quirked upward. "I'd say I was right."

Scott stared at him. Hesitated, then decided the man deserved it. "I…I used to think your family was lucky. Even with what happened to your dad, they were lucky. Because they had you."

Chief Highwater looked surprised, and Scott had the sudden feeling that for all his achievements, the man was as humble as he'd ever been. A man who'd had to step up when his family needed him, and who had done just that in an exemplary fashion. And succeeded in building a family that was rock solid, everyone united, no matter what life threw at them.

The kind of family he had never had.

Scott handed him the big envelope. "The judge told me this says all that needs to be said."

As the chief looked at the file Scott didn't sit in the offered chair but stood at ease, hands clasped behind him. It seemed appropriate somehow, this military posture, in front of this man. When he had finished, the chief looked up. He was smiling. Widely.

"Nicely done, Marine. You truly found that path."

Scott took a breath. "None of it would have happened if you hadn't gone to bat for me."

"You needed someone to."

"I never expected that. Especially from…you."

The man didn't speak for a moment, just looked at him assessingly. Then, with a very different sort of smile, he said, "Do you know why I did it?"

Scott blinked. "I…the judge said you told him I just needed a path, a goal."

The chief nodded. "And I believed that. But do you know why I did it?" Frowning, Scott shook his head. "Because I listened to one of the most impassioned and convincing speeches I've ever heard. An explanation of the facet of your family that no one really knew, of your parents and your brothers pulling so tightly together to fight Peter's disease that you were shut out, abandoned as surely as if they'd tossed you out on the street. Left to your own devices when they weren't verbally abusing you or literally shoving you out of the way. All because you weren't a donor match for your brother. Which was the reason you were conceived in the first place."

A chill had begun to overtake Scott at the first sentence. It grew, enveloping him, a hideous feeling of shame and embarrassment. Not simply because the man knew, that he'd been the useless brother, the dud, the first attempt that had failed, and so instead of being supportive he'd gone haywire, acted out every chance he got. That was bad enough, but even worse was the simple fact that he knew how Sergeant Highwater had learned all this. Because only one person in Last Stand had ever known.

Sage.

She'd betrayed his confidence. She'd spilled his secrets, spilled it all. But...for his sake.

...one of the most impassioned and convincing speeches I've ever heard.

Sage. Sage had been the one to fight for him. Fighting for him even when he no longer had the strength to do it himself.

She'd always been the one. The only one.

He was dimly aware that he'd sat in the chair opposite the desk. Had the vague thought he was lucky he hadn't missed it and ended up on the floor.

He should have had that drink.

SCOTT WAS BARELY aware of leaving the police station. He hadn't even been aware of which way he'd been walking until he looked up and realized he was passing the elementary school.

At least we'll be rid of him half the day now.

His father's words, uttered to his mother the first day they'd brought him here, echoed in his head. He hadn't gotten it then, but he'd only been five. It had been later, when the teacher had told another child to take that sticky candy wrapper and "get rid of it, it's only trash," that he'd understood. That's what he was to them, just trash, something to get rid of.

And a few years later, when he'd found that adoption paperwork stashed in a drawer, he'd understood just how serious they'd been. They'd tried to make it sound like it was for his own good, that with their deathly ill oldest they couldn't take care of him, too, but he knew better. They'd been more than able—and willing—to take care of Robbie, when it turned out he was the match Pete needed.

A police unit cruised by, slowly. The same woman as before. Curious, as before. No, more curious, maybe because he was standing staring at a school full of little kids. She pulled to the curb. He sighed inwardly, knowing if he took off now it would only look more suspicious. So here he was, once more about to be interrogated by a Last Stand cop. Just like old times.

She was a petite thing who only came up to his shoulder, with short, sandy blond hair that looked windblown, and large, dark brown eyes. Soft, doe eyes, the guys he'd served with would call them, the kind that made you feel protective. But this woman looked fit and strong, and moved with a kind of ease that told him she could probably hold her own long enough to get some big doofus handcuffed, at least. And she certainly didn't hesitate to approach him.

He remembered Sage telling him that when she was fifteen Shane had taught her, just as he'd taught Sean, how to handle an assailant who was bigger than her, how to use her opponent's height and weight and assumptions against him. Scott had the feeling his siblings weren't the only ones her brother had taught, or at least made sure they knew what they needed to know to give them the best chance.

"Looking for something?" Her voice was calm, her tone merely inquisitive. Her name tag read E. Stratton.

"At something," he said. He nodded toward the school. "I went there."

She looked him up and down more intently. "So did I. Did you have Mr. Stults?"

Clever, he thought. "Don't know him. I had Mrs. Washington in kindergarten, Mr. Matta my last year, and some I don't remember much in between."

She relaxed, for the most part. "I had Mr. Matta, too. Tough guy, but fair." He wouldn't argue with that. The man had been one of the few who had taken time with him, told him he was smart, he just needed to apply himself. He hadn't believed him. Officer Stratton studied him again for a moment. "I must have been ahead of you."

His mouth quirked. "Most people were."

She chuckled, and relaxed the rest of the way. She was

actually rather cute, once the steely demeanor eased.

"Officer Stratton!" The call came from behind them, a rather shrill female voice. He looked, thought the woman seemed familiar. Or the voice, maybe.

"Mrs. Murray," the woman in uniform said with a nod, her expression unreadable.

Scott groaned inwardly as the name brought it all back. The teacher he'd put out of his mind most. The one who had sat in judgment on him from his first day in her class, and never let him forget she found him sadly wanting. The woman he'd hidden from any time he saw her until he'd moved on to middle school, and even then, since it was practically next door, he'd kept an eye out for her.

"I'm so glad you caught him," the woman, who had to be in her sixties now, said as she hastened toward them. "Has he already done something or were you able to stop him?"

He drew in a breath and turned to face the woman. "Nice to know you remember me, Mrs. Murray," he said politely.

She looked startled, but the scowl returned quickly. "I heard you were back for your poor brother's funeral. I can't imagine why you came, when you're not wanted."

"I'm wondering myself," he muttered.

The woman ignored him and turned back to Officer Stratton. "I know he was gone before you came here, but you should be warned. He's a horrible troublemaker, always was. Fighting, stealing, probably worse, and all with his poor family needing him to be supportive. They never should have let him avoid jail like they did."

He saw the officer's gaze shift to him. "I wouldn't argue with the first part," he said quietly.

"Avoided jail?" Officer Stratton asked. "A deal?"

"Marines. Ten years."

"You're out now?"

He nodded. "Honorably," he added.

"Then I'd say you've paid your fellow citizens back and then some," she said.

Mrs. Murray scoffed. "Some people never change."

He turned to look at his old nemesis again, rather pointedly. "I wouldn't argue that, either."

She gave an inelegant snort, warned the officer to keep an eye on him, and turned to walk back into the classroom where she was no doubt terrorizing a new batch of kids.

Some people never did change.

Neither did some places.

And the determination to get everything he had to do done so he could be out of here as soon as possible rose up again. And forget waiting until Sunday, he'd head back to Austin and the airport the instant that funeral was over. See if he could change the flight, or if not, stay there overnight.

He'd do whatever he had to, to get out of Last Stand faster.

SAGE RESISTED THROWING her arms around Poke's neck and hugging him, but only because she knew the horse would give her the side eye if she did. A good, solid slap on the neck, or even a kiss on the nose was all right, but the big dun drew the line at blatant embraces.

"We're going to show them in Oklahoma," she told him as she turned him loose in the big corral so he could, as she knew he would, go find a nice dusty spot to roll in. She didn't even care that she'd just groomed him. Not after the performance he'd turned in during their workout this morning. Every time she decided the horse had reached his peak, he went a little further, until the phrase "The sky's the limit" was all she could think of. He was going to blind them with his brilliance at the national competition in Oklahoma City in June.

She heard the signal from the speaker that hung over the main door of the barn, announcing that someone was coming through the gate out at the road. Someone who had the code, since it was the chime of the gate opening, not the buzz asking for entry. Lily, maybe; she was the most likely to be free during the day. Whichever of the family it was, she was glad once more that Sean had rigged the system for her, so she wouldn't miss it if she was outside.

This time when she thought of her brother she felt an unwanted wistfulness. She'd accepted that being the youngest meant she'd probably be the last to find what her brothers had found, but her record had been pretty miserable so far, her longest relationship a three-month adventure with a bull rider from Omaha that had ended exactly as she'd expected, a gradual fading away rather than an official termination. Which had been fitting, since the relationship hadn't really been worth fighting for, emotionally or physically.

But then, she'd only ever had one that had been.

So here she was at twenty-six, not having had even a date since that disaster with Dan Hockney, and—

"Stop moping," she ordered herself sternly. She'd heard the vehicle on the drive, and needed to pull herself together before whoever it was got here. The last thing she wanted was Lily zeroing in on her and demanding to know what was wrong. Her brothers, at least, would be wary enough not to ask. Besides, she had no qualms about telling them to butt out.

She knew what had brought on all this introspection. And how bad was it when just the thought of the boy she'd had such a consuming crush on in high school could bring this on ten years after he'd vanished from Last Stand and her life without a word?

Really bad. And you'd better start thinking about how you're going to deal if he does show up for the funeral, and you run into him. Cool and disinterested? Bitter and angry?

She grimaced to herself. Chided herself for assuming he'd even remember or recognize her if she did see him. Which she could, with some planning, easily avoid. It wasn't like she'd go to the funeral. It was cold of her, she supposed, but she had no desire to pretend to honor the guy who was an ass in the first place who had then made years of sacrifice and pain and torment pointless by getting drunk and driving into a freaking lake. The only people she really felt bad for were Robbie, the brother who had been the sacrificial lamb as it were, and…Scott.

Scott, who had been pushed aside because he was useless

to them.

Scott, who had tried to help but been soundly rejected.

Scott, who at ten had figured out the only reason he existed. That he was a futile try for, as he'd put it later at sixteen, "spare parts."

Scott, who had refused to take her virginity, despite obvious evidence he wanted her and she'd practically begged him to, because he thought he wasn't good enough for her.

Scott, who—

She stopped with a gasp.

Scott, who was getting out of the car that had stopped just ten feet away.

Scott, who had clearly become every inch the man she'd known he would. Tall, powerful, broad-shouldered, and narrow-hipped.

Scott, with a strong, masculine jaw that made her fingers curl.

Scott, with those green eyes that had so fascinated her, eyes that now looked as if they'd seen too far and too much.

Scott, who left me without a word and never looked back. Didn't care enough to even let me know he was alive.

She wouldn't grant him bitterness, but anger? Yeah, that she could do. She headed for him with full intent to do…something. And maybe it wouldn't involve the knife she always kept in her boot while outside.

Or maybe it would.

Chapter Five

SAGE HIGHWATER WASN'T the girl he'd left all those years ago. Oh, she was still visible, in the long, silky dark hair, and those vivid blue eyes rimmed with thick, dark lashes were unmistakable. But this was a woman. The reed-thin slenderness had rounded just enough, in a very female way, and her mouth was...lusher somehow. Even the way she moved was different, not her stride, which was still long and confident and emphasized by the slim leather chaps she wore, but in the slightest sway that hadn't been there before.

Scott had the sudden, heat-inducing thought that he should be damned glad she was walking toward him, because watching her walk away, in those jeans, would be a major exercise in self-control.

Belatedly he realized that those blue eyes didn't hold welcome. And a sudden memory of the fiery temper he'd glimpsed more than once hit him. Back then, it had amazed him simply because it was unleashed mostly in his defense, such a novelty to him he hadn't been sure how to deal with it.

But now it apparently was aimed at him, and he was even less sure how to deal. And he realized with a bit of wry self-knowledge that he'd faced armed insurgents that rattled him less.

He'd had his doubts when Shane had told him where she was and given him the gate code. But after what he'd said, how could he deny that the one he most needed to thank for saving his life was not the judge or the chief, but the girl who had stood up for him when no one else would?

She came to a halt in front of him. He saw the glint in her eye and instinctively gauged the distance between them, and whether he could dodge if she took a swing at him. But he knew he wouldn't, even if she did take that swing. Because he deserved to take that hit, from her.

She didn't take the swing. She just stood there, glaring at him.

But beneath the glare, the obvious anger, he saw a hint of the girl she'd been. And he remembered the first day she'd ever exploded on him, when they'd met at that place along Hickory Creek east of the high school, on the Buckley property, the spot where a ledge of limestone jutted out over the water, and they could sit. And talk. As he'd never talked to anyone before or since.

He'd been late that day, but she'd waited. And when she'd seen his face, and the result of his mother backhanding him with the hand that bore the flashy ruby ring that was almost the same color as the bloody scratch it had left, she'd erupted. She'd been furiously, gloriously angry, and he'd been filled with a feeling he couldn't even put a name to, that it was for him. That he'd been trying to stand up for Robbie, who had been crying in his room when they'd told him there would be more painful procedures, hadn't mattered to his mother at all, but it had mattered to Sage. It had taken every bit of persuasion he had in him to get her not to charge off and tell her cop brother, which was the last thing he wanted, to give them another reason to hate him.

And the memory made his throat tight and his voice rough when he said, "Why do I think saying you're beautiful when you're angry would likely get me killed?"

"Because it would," she answered, and he heard the slightest of tremors in her voice, just enough to suggest there might be something besides anger boiling inside her. When he realized it was pain, he felt his gut knot.

"Sage—"

"What are you doing here?"

"Believe me, Last Stand is the last place I want to be. I'll be out of here as soon as they start tossing dirt on the coffin, and it still won't be soon enough."

"I don't mean that. I mean here." She stamped a boot on the ground. He'd forgotten how small and delicate seeming her feet were, on a girl as tall as she was. "On *my* ranch."

He blinked. "Your ranch?"

"It's mine in the most important sense. I run it. The family voted it that way."

"But that's…a full-time job."

Her brow furrowed. "So?"

"But…you're a police officer, right?"

She went very still. "No. I'm not."

He stared at her. "You're not? But you were always going to—"

"Things change, all right? I got through the academy, proved I could do it, then—" She stopped herself, only to begin with that full head of steam again. "Why am I explaining to you? To you of all people, who won't even explain what you're doing here!"

"I...your brother sent me."

"And gave you the gate code? Which brother? I'll chew a hole in his hide."

"Please don't," he said warily.

"Which one?" she demanded again.

"The chief."

Sage blinked. Damn, those eyes were amazing. "Shane?" He didn't think he was imagining that some of the intensity of her anger receded. Such was the power of Shane Highwater, even with his volatile little sister. "Why?"

He'd thought about what to say. Figured he'd better have the words ready, before she distracted him from what he needed to get said. So they came out in a bit of a rush.

"I went to see him. To thank him. Until Judge Morales told me, I never knew he was the one who interceded for me with the judge, and the recruiter. And then he told me why he did it. That it was you, that you went to bat for me, fiercely." He swallowed. And added in a voice that was rough again because of the knot in his throat, "Like you always did."

Her head came up sharply. "And what did that get me? Why, it got me you leaving without a backward glance."

"I didn't know you'd done it," he protested.

For some reason that seemed to make her anger spike

again. It may have been ten years, but he still recognized the danger in her tone when she said, far too carefully, "So if you had known, you'd have come to say goodbye?"

If there was anything he'd learned since the day he'd left Last Stand behind him—he'd thought forever—it was that knowing you were stepping into a minefield and doing it anyway was tantamount to suicide. So he said nothing, hoping it would prod her into saying something that would help him understand.

It did.

"What we had wasn't enough on its own for you to even bother?"

He got it then. He closed his eyes, unable to bear the anger and yes, the pain, in those eyes another second. He opened his mouth to speak, to try to explain, but no words would come. And this time she just waited, silently. The girl he'd known had never managed that. She, too, had changed. For the better, or worse? He didn't know. But if it was worse, he knew who was responsible.

Finally he made himself look at her again. "I never meant to hurt you."

"Too little, too late, Parrish."

"Sage, listen, I tried—"

"Sure. Go."

"I did—"

"Don't let the gate hit you on your way out."

She turned on her heel and walked away. Toward the big, sprawling ranch house, not the barn. Probably so she could lock the doors on him, he thought. But then he couldn't think at all, because he was confronted with what he'd been afraid of from the moment he'd gotten here; the sight of Sage Highwater, a very womanly Sage Highwater, walking away from him in those tight jeans, with that feminine sway and a sweet little backside that made his fingers curl until they dug into his palms.

More memories swamped him, of that night he'd snuck out of the house after dark—although not much sneaking was required, since they'd long since quit paying any attention to his whereabouts—and met her at that spot. Their spot. She'd had to be more careful sneaking out, although since she'd saddled up and ridden one of the Highwater horses she'd been able to make a nice, quiet exit.

It had taken her a while, since their ranch was farther away, far enough that she normally rode the bus to school. She'd slid out of the saddle and into his arms, and had been kissing him before her feet even touched the ground. That had been the night things had nearly careened out of control, when the feel of her, the taste of her, had sent every already raging teenage hormone into overdrive. When she'd pulled a condom out of her pocket—he never did find out who she'd "borrowed" it from—he'd nearly lost it.

It had taken everything he had in him back then to say no. To tell her that the only thing he wanted more than what she was offering was not to have her brothers hunting him down. Again.

He stood there staring at the door she'd closed behind her, and no doubt locked. But he wasn't seeing the door, or the house. Because he was back to that day, with the discussion they'd had echoing in his mind as if it had just happened.

"What do you mean, again?"

He'd given her a wry look. "Do you really think they haven't already? That your cop brother especially hasn't warned me off?" *And rightfully so. I'm no good for the likes of a Highwater.*

She looked as if it honestly hadn't occurred to her that her protective brother might see something amiss with her getting too close to the kind of screwup he was. But she said determinedly, "I'll tell Shane to butt out."

"He's just looking out for you."

"I'm not a child anymore," she'd said spiritedly, getting to her feet as if she were ready to race back home and chew out her big brother. "He needs to back off."

"Sage, don't." He'd tried to bite back the next words, but as they so often did with her, they came tumbling out anyway. "Be glad he gives a damn, all right? You've got brothers who love you, look out for you. That's more than a lot of people have."

She had stopped dead then, and sank back down to sit beside him. "You have brothers," she said quietly.

"Do I?" He hadn't meant it to sound so bitter, so pitiful, but this girl, this livewire, seemed to open up every door to every deep, dark space in his head.

"Yes," she insisted. "Maybe they're far from perfect, but you still have them. Don't wish them away."

"They're not like your brothers," he'd tried to explain. "They…they're complete, together. They don't need me.

They never have. I don't matter to them."

"Like Kane doesn't matter to my brothers." She'd let out a huge sigh. "I got out his guitar yesterday, because…I needed to. To touch something that had been precious to him. To think about how well he played it, how beautiful his voice is. They told me to put it away. And when I wouldn't, they just left the room."

He'd felt a jab of regret for letting that particular door open. Not for his own sake, because he couldn't imagine anything that would change his lack of relationship with his siblings, but because he knew she knew what she was talking about. Because the same day she'd lost her beloved father, she'd also lost her other brother, Kane. Lost him amid a cloud of speculation on exactly what he'd had to do with that father's death. And Kane had been the brother she'd been closest to, both in age and connection. The brother who'd made up a song for her when she was little, about her bluebonnet eyes.

He hadn't known what to say to that, then. He'd been so mired in his own misery he selfishly hadn't really thought about hers, or even seriously considered the possibility that Sage Highwater's life wasn't the shining ideal he'd always thought it must be.

But now she had to know better, had to know her brothers had never stopped looking for the missing one. Which only proved his other point: the Highwater brothers were very, very different than his own.

He snapped out of the reverie, feeling oddly like he was being watched. It was a sensation he hadn't had since he'd left combat zones behind, but it still made the hair on the back of his neck stand on end. He looked around, half expecting to see one of the Highwater brothers heading at him, possibly locked and loaded. But the only living things he saw were a couple of scrub jays in the tree next to the barn, and the big horse in the corral.

Who was, in fact, staring at him.

"What are you, her guard horse?" he muttered.

The horse snorted and bobbed his head as if he were nodding an affirmative.

Okay, you're losing it, Parrish. It's a horse.

But something about the big brown eyes drew him and he walked over to the animal. And stood there for a moment, wishing the big creature could tell him what to do. He glanced back at the silent ranch house. He wondered idly if all the Highwaters still lived there; she'd told him once that their father had planned it that way, turning the place into separate, private wings for each of them, joined at one common area. She, he knew, had the upstairs all to herself.

And what would she do if he didn't leave? Come out armed and ready? It wouldn't surprise him.

And for the first time he was glad he was going to be here for a couple of days. Because he still hadn't actually managed to get out the words, "Thank you." He owed her that.

And he was damned well going to leave Last Stand debt free.

Chapter Six

SAGE SAT IN the middle of her bed with her knees drawn up, her arms wrapped around them, and her chin resting on her right kneecap. She'd toed off her boots, but only because she'd just washed her comforter after she'd inadvertently flipped a slice of pizza face down on it.

She made herself breathe, concentrated on it, in and out. This because she'd caught herself holding her breath while waiting for the sound of his car leaving. It finally came, but long after she would have expected after her abrupt and cold dismissal.

But what else was she supposed to do? He had as much as admitted that the only reason he'd come was because he'd found out she'd gone to bat for him back then. Proving that their relationship alone hadn't been enough for him to feel he owed her at least a goodbye.

Relationship. Right.

Apparently they hadn't really had one. Or at least, not the kind she'd thought they had. All those hours by the creek, talking, hadn't meant what she'd thought they had.

But she finally had the answer to the one thing she'd never been able to fully decide. When he'd first gone, and when she'd first faced the truth of where he was going, what he'd be doing, and the very real chance he might die doing it, she'd regretted with all her sixteen-year-old heart that she hadn't pushed him into making love to her.

Now she was damned glad she hadn't.

Or was she? Because if she was certain of nothing else, she was sure sex with Scott would have been incendiary. It would have been nice to have her first time have been like that, and not the fumbling, inept thing it had been her first year in college.

Incendiary. Oh, yes. Because even now, just looking at him kicked up her pulse and heated places long unheard from. At seventeen, he'd been tall, but rather wiry in a quicksilver sort of way. She'd always wondered if he was thin because they didn't feed him. But now he'd not just filled out, he'd become solid, having grown into his height and breadth of shoulder. He was muscled, but more like a racehorse than Poke's quarter horse bulk. He just looked strong. Fit. Tough…beautiful.

Damn his hide anyway.

Why did he have to be the only one who'd ever stirred her this way? Why did he have to have those vivid, deep green eyes she felt like she could get lost in for days? Why was he the one who had been able to get to her with just a sideways look, that almost shy, endearing look that melted her every time? And now, now that he was no longer that boy but a man, and a man with both power and grace…

And confidence.

Her head came up as that thought struck her. She

thought, decided it was true. She hadn't seen any trace of the shy, hesitant boy in the man who had turned up here today.

But he'd gone. He hadn't followed her, tried to get her to let him in.

Sage nearly laughed at herself then. She'd ordered him to go, and now she was feeling whiny when he did as she'd asked?

Did you really think he'd persist, when he didn't even care enough to say goodbye ten years ago?

When she caught herself rocking back and forth, as she had in the days right after her father had died, she froze. And she turned that biting tone she had used on him on herself.

"Stop brooding and get moving, Highwater. You've got work to do. Nobody's got time for your whining."

She would not, after all, have to see him again. She would simply avoid going into town until after the funeral; she was sure he meant it when he'd said he'd leave right after. She was a little surprised he'd actually come in the first place. She wondered if, in his position, she would have come to the funeral of the man who had sucked up every bit of caring in a family that apparently didn't have enough love to go around.

The whole thing was such a waste. No, worse, it was a farce, and a bad farce, that a man who had been given so much, who had, with years of help from a small army of doctors and a sibling—who'd had no choice in the matter—defeated a pernicious illness, had then thrown away the life that had been saved. Made all the sacrifice for nothing, dying in a stupid, drunk-driving car crash at thirty-two.

"Stop it." She ordered herself to stop thinking about it, stop thinking about him, as she pulled her boots back on and headed back downstairs to finish her day's work. It had taken her a very long time before, to train herself not to think about him. But she had, and she could do it again now. This was just a minor blip on the radar. And the final one, she was sure.

THE MOMENT HE stepped into the saloon, Scott nearly turned tail and ran. He hadn't expected that a Highwater would still be running the place. When he'd left, the eldest, now chief brother was already a cop, the next was off at some fancy eastern school, the next already in the police academy, and the youngest was two years missing.

And Sage had been sixteen and hurting. Thanks to you.

He clamped down on that thought, isolated it, shoved it aside. Decided if he started running now, he'd never stop.

"Shane mentioned you were here. Been wondering if I'd see you," the man behind the bar said as he neared.

Even if he had known a Highwater still ran this place, he never would have expected it to be this one. And he was even more surprised the man seemed to recognize him. But Scott knew him; he remembered Sage's youthful wish that she'd had this brother's unique, turquoise eyes. He'd told her he wouldn't trade her bluebonnet blue eyes for anything.

"Mr. Highwater," he said.

Those eyes looked him up and down. "I think we can

dispense with the mister, Scott. Unless you prefer Mr. Parrish."

Scott let out a snort before he could stop it. "Mr. Parrish is my father."

"And that," Slater Highwater said, "is no recommendation, is it." It wasn't a question, which was a good thing because Scott was too startled to answer. "What'll you have this afternoon? First one's on the house."

Scott blinked. "What?"

"First one always is, for our military."

He smiled at that. "Thanks. But...I'm not anymore."

"But you weren't here while you were, so it still holds. So, what? Maybe a shooter of Outlaw and a beer?"

"That's two drinks, technically."

The man behind the bar grinned. "My bad. But I'm committed now."

Scott grinned back, feeling easier now. "Done," he said. "Outlaw? They're still here?"

"Not just here. The Delaneys have built it into a pretty well-known label."

As he watched the man deftly pour the two-stage drink he said, "I always had the idea the Highwaters and the Delaneys didn't get along."

"Those are the law enforcement Highwaters," Slater said.

"Which you're not."

"No more than you're the miscreant you once were. With good reason," the man added as he pushed the shot glass and the cold beer across the bar to him.

Scott stared at the other man. "Good reason? What the

hell do you know about it?" Then the obvious hit him. "Sage."

The second, by all accounts brilliant Highwater brother didn't dissemble. "Yes."

The image of Sage, her bluebonnet eyes flashing with anger, slammed back into his mind. "I'm surprised you're even talking to me," he muttered.

"I can't deny you leaving hurt her, badly."

"I had no choice."

"I know that, too. And so does she."

"Then why is she so pissed at me?"

The man behind the bar raised a brow at him. "Is she?"

Scott sighed. "Yeah. I just came from your ranch."

"Hmm."

Well that was helpful. Although why he thought anything or anyone—especially another Highwater—would help, he had no idea. He was almost grateful when the cell phone on the bar let out a notification. He thought he recognized the few notes of a song, but couldn't put a name to it.

Slater Highwater smiled widely, picking it up without even looking at the screen. "You found today's note." A pause. Scott wondered if that meant the man wrote some kind of note every day. "I meant every word, Joey my love." Another pause, during which the man's smile became a rakish grin. "Indeed we will. I look forward to it."

That kind of note, then. Scott felt a tiny prod of…something, at the pure love that echoed in the man's voice. And then as Slater put the phone back down something else hit him. "Joey?"

"Joey Douglas. You remember her?"

"Yeah. I remember her readings, at the library and the Bluebonnet Festival."

"She's the assistant librarian now."

"I'm not surprised. She was really good."

"She still is," Slater said, with that same grin.

Okay, so the little jab had been envy. He grimaced. "Obviously notes work better for you than me."

"Helps that my lady loves words."

"And quotes? I remember Sage saying you always had one for any occasion."

Slater looked pleased at that. "That, too. For instance," he said, again looking at Scott assessingly, "for you I'd quote Seneca."

He was too intrigued not to ask. "Ancient Roman, right?"

Slater smiled. "Sage always said you were much smarter than your grades showed."

Scott shrugged. "I just didn't give a damn. Then."

Slater nodded. "Seneca was a stoic. And I thought of this quote of his because it could only be said about someone the direct opposite of you."

Scott hesitated, but after a moment said, "I'll bite. What quote?"

"'I judge you unfortunate because you have never lived through misfortune. You have passed through life without an opponent—no one can ever know what you are capable of, not even you.'"

For a long, silent moment Scott stared at the man, feeling both embarrassed, and complimented, a combination he'd felt few times in his life. Then, slowly, he said, "Aren't you one of the brothers who warned me off your little sister?"

"I warned the boy you were. And, I might add, before I understood why you were that boy."

He almost flushed. The last thing he wanted—from anyone, but especially a Highwater—was pity. "Sage talked too much," he muttered.

He reached for the shooter and downed it in a gulp. Let the tequila hit. It had been a while, so the punch was noticeable. He waited, savoring the taste; Outlaw Tequila definitely had this down. Then he finally went for a long draw on the beer.

"So," Slater said as he wiped down a glass, "who did your notes not work on?"

That caught him off guard enough to answer. Rather sourly. "More like a letter. Singular. And your sister. Since she's still pissed at me ten years later, I think it's safe to assume it didn't work, don't you?"

Slater drew back slightly. "Wait. Are you saying you wrote her when you left?"

His head came up then. "I did. About three pages' worth. Or worthless, I guess. Spent hours on it."

"Sage never said anything about a letter."

"Maybe she didn't even read it. If she's still this angry now, she must have been furious then. Enough to have just burned it or something."

"Neither of my brothers mentioned a letter arriving, either."

"I…didn't mail it. I was afraid you guys wouldn't give it to her."

Slater seemed to ponder that. "We would never have withheld it, but given your experience I can understand why you'd think that. So what did you do, slip it into her locker at school or something?"

He shook his head. "I didn't want to set foot on campus again. Ever."

"Then what, Scott? I was here at the time. And she very plainly said you left without a word of any kind to her. Never even said goodbye." Slater set down the glass. "Which rather ticked me off, I might add. You were the third huge blow in her life. Mother, father, and then you."

He swallowed tightly at that. "But…" He trailed off, puzzled now. Could it be she'd never found it? But how could she miss it? He'd left it in the place she herself had pointed out as the perfect hiding place.

"I think," Slater said, "perhaps you need to talk to her again. You owe her that much." Scott stood up and pushed the barstool back. Then Slater added mildly, "Just a reminder. She is a very good shot."

Scott looked up and held the other man's gaze steadily. "I don't try to be a target anymore."

"Good." He'd turned to go when Slater spoke again. Softly. "Seneca also said 'Sometimes even to live is an act of courage.'"

Scott stopped in his tracks. Looked back. Saw the quiet understanding in the eyes Sage had coveted.

Scott nodded. And feeling as if he'd been saluted, he headed for the door. And all the way back to the car he pondered the oddity of having two of the Highwater brothers apparently now approving of him.

Chapter Seven

H E WAS BACK.
Sage knew it midswing of her hammer, well before she turned to look, knew it because she could feel him, as if his mere presence awoke senses in her that no one else did. Or could.

And that made her decide not to look at all, for fear it would all show in her face, that she had never forgotten one tiny thing about him. She remembered it all, from the way his eyes had darkened to a deep forest green when he wore that shirt he'd had in the same shade, to the way his hair grew, and the thick, soft eyelashes more than one girl had coveted.

Suddenly the fence board she'd been replacing became less heavy. He'd moved to hold it. She drove the nail home with one blow that had everything she was feeling behind it. Then she turned on him.

"I didn't need your help."

"You never did. It was me who needed yours."

He said it so simply, so easily she stared at him. How many times back then had he declared, angrily, that he didn't need her help or anyone else's? But she'd known it had come out of pain, because she'd felt it herself then, and still felt it now. The gaping hole in her life was the absence of her father and brother. In his, it was the absence of…everything.

When she'd realized the extent of his family's abandonment of him, it had been the first step toward healing for her, because she realized that even after her father's death, thanks to her brothers, she still had more love and caring in her life than he had ever had.

When she didn't speak, he grimaced and said, "Your brother sent me back here."

"Again?"

"Different brother."

Her brow furrowed for an instant. "Slater," she said, knowing Sean was over in Stonewall, serving an arrest warrant. "Needed a drink, huh?"

She saw his gaze narrow over her tone. She'd worried about it back then, although she'd never seen him seriously out of control. And she understood he did it to dull the pain.

"Half my allotment of two," he said. "And that's only when I do. Which isn't often. Hasn't been for years."

So she'd gotten to him with that. She'd always been able to tell when she had. He might be older, more impressive, but she could still tell. She wasn't sure how it made her feel, either that she could still tell, or that she could still get to him. But if he meant that about limiting himself to an occasional two drinks, she was glad to hear it. It hadn't escalated as she had once feared it would. He must have finally realized booze only masked the pain, that underneath it was still there and ready to strike.

She tossed her hammer back in the toolbox at her feet and turned to face him head-on, her arms crossed in front of her. She was sure some body language expert would have something to say about her posture.

"What did Slater say? That I'm supposed to listen to you after you left like that? You couldn't manage even a voice mail?"

He frowned slightly. "I wouldn't use their phone, and I didn't have a cell phone, you knew that."

She had known, because she'd offered him hers more than once when he'd said his parents weren't about to waste that kind of money on him. "You could have found a way. But no, you left without a word. Not. A. Freaking. Word, Scott Parrish."

When he looked at her then his eyes were intent, and his voice was very quiet when he said, "You never found the letter."

She nearly snarled. "Bull. I haunted our mailbox for weeks. You never sent me any letter."

"Not sent, no. I knew your brothers didn't want me…around you, so I thought they'd intercept it. So I left it for you to find. At our spot on the creek." She stared at him. Even she wasn't sure if it was with more anger, or disbelief. "I did," he insisted. "Remember that fissure in the limestone, right where we used to sit? The one you said would be a good place to hide something?"

Sage felt an instant chill. She felt suddenly short of air, and her chest hurt almost too much to breathe. Then, slowly, she whispered, "I never went back there. I couldn't. It hurt too much."

She heard him swear under his breath. It was a moment before he said, in a tone that almost matched hers, "You really believed I left without a word? Without ever telling you what you and those stolen times beside the creek meant to me? What they did for me?"

"You really…wrote me a letter?"

"I may not have always told you everything, Sage, but I have never lied to you."

"Yes, you did."

He blinked, drew back. "I never—"

"All those times you told me you were all right, when I knew you weren't."

"Oh."

She could tell by the almost sheepish change in his expression that he hadn't thought of that as a lie, and maybe it wasn't in the strictest sense, but she'd known it wasn't true. He wasn't all right. So many times he'd said it, and she'd known he wasn't.

She stared at him anew—now not in anger or hurt, but assessingly. Cataloging with more attention this time the changes in the boy she'd once known and loved. She'd already noticed the increased muscle, although he still moved with the same easy grace. He seemed a little taller, and she wondered if it was simply that he was standing tall now, no longer beaten down. He was taut, broad-shouldered, and clearly fit, and she'd be willing to bet there was a nice set of abs under that long-sleeved T-shirt.

His hands—was it odd that she noticed this?—were still strong-looking, with long fingers that no doubt made it easy for him to handle whatever weapon they gave him. His hair where it was still fairly short was that same sandy brown, but the top, a little bit longer, was tipped with a golden, nearly blond color, as if it had been lightened by the summer sun.

Or the desert sun.

Sage felt a jolt of guilt. She'd been so personally angry she'd practically forgotten where he'd been and what he'd done. She, who so fiercely honored and saluted the men who fought, had completely ignored that in her private pain. And she didn't like that she'd done it.

"I'm sorry," she said, meaning it despite the fact that it came out rather stiffly. "I let my personal feelings get in the way of welcoming a member of the military home. Thank you for your service."

He drew back as sharply as if she'd slapped him. He stared at her for a long, silent moment. Then, in a voice as emotionless as the fence board he'd held, he said, "Don't bother."

Before she could even react he'd turned on his heel and strode back to his car. The back tires kicked up a small spray of dirt as he wheeled the vehicle sharply around and left the way he had come.

She stared after him, wondering what on earth had brought that on. And it was a long, silent minute or two of her own before her mind went back to what he'd told her.

And she wondered what that letter had said.

SCOTT REALIZED WHEN he blew past the marker post showing the water depth in case of flooding and hit the big dip on the ranch road, and the car protested with a heavy jolt that rattled his teeth, that he was driving too fast. He drew in a long, slow breath as he slowed down.

Thank you for your service.

It wasn't that he minded the words so much, not as some of his brothers in arms did. But Scott knew that people who honestly felt that way needed to say it. That those same people were likely those who contributed to organizations that helped veterans and guys who hadn't come back as whole as he had. And he was glad they said it; it was nice to hear and he appreciated it, although he wasn't sure he deserved it given how his military career began.

No, he didn't mind the words or the sentiment at all.

What he minded was them coming from Sage. Because those words were what someone who didn't know anything about you except what the uniform signified said. What someone who had no idea who you were out of that uniform said. They were words from a stranger.

Not words from the girl who'd once been the only life preserver the universe had ever thrown his teenaged self.

Not words from the girl who'd once made him wonder what to call this strange feeling he experienced every time he saw her.

The girl who'd made him wonder if it was what they called love.

Chapter Eight

"How'd it go?"

Sage looked at her oldest brother over the rim of the coffee mug. It was her third cup this morning, before she'd even set foot outside. It still wasn't going to be enough after the sleepless night she'd had. Every time she'd managed to stop wondering what had set him off, she started wondering about that letter. She'd spent a moment or two wondering if it was true, but in her gut she knew it was. He hadn't just vanished without a word, she just hadn't found the words he'd left. Because she'd been hurt too badly to revisit the place where they'd spent so many hours together.

Coward. Some Highwater you are.

"Sage?"

She smothered a sigh. Thought about playing dumb and saying, "How'd what go?" But this was Shane, and that would never fly with him. But she kept the letter part to herself, for the moment.

"You didn't have to send him out to thank me."

"I didn't. I just told him what you told me ten years ago. He's the one who realized who he really needed to thank."

"I only told you the truth."

"And changed his life in the process. He took that chance you gave him and ran with it. Farther than I ever thought he would or could."

She drew back slightly. "What do you mean?"

Shane raised a brow at her. "He didn't show you?"

"Show me what?" Surely he hadn't kept a copy of that letter all this time?

"His military record," Shane said, looking puzzled now.

She felt her cheeks heat and raised her mug to her lips again, hoping the warmth from the coffee would explain the pink that was no doubt showing. "No," she muttered and took a sip. *Because I didn't give him the chance.*

"Well, he should have," Shane said, looking curious in that way that had never boded well for keeping a secret from him. And still didn't; he might be the chief now, but he was ever and always a cop at heart. The only thing worse than having him after something she wanted to keep hidden would be having Sean after it.

"He never mentioned anything about his…service." She tried not to stumble over the word as the question of what had set him off poked at her again.

"He should have," Shane repeated, gently now. "It's beyond impressive. He won the Bronze Star, Sage. That's…" Shane's voice faded away and he shook his head as if he had no words.

She stared at her brother, and she truly did have no words for what she was feeling. After a moment, Shane went on.

"He not only made rank, he became a Scout Sniper. A

combination unique to the Marine Corps, I understand, and a very difficult thing to achieve. I did a little research, and the other branches separate the two, but not the Marines. You have to be an expert at both. Concealment, stalking and the like, as well as the shooting."

Sage blinked; he'd snagged her brain back on one word. "He was a sniper?"

"Had a list of medals and commendations a couple of pages long. And he shot competitively, with another list of shooting gold medals. Including something called the National Interservice Rifle Competition. Was accepted for additional training at the Israeli Sniper School." Shane's mouth quirked. "I wouldn't want to go up against him."

She stared at her brother. "You really did do some research."

"I saw the record, but I wanted to know how to interpret it all. That Bronze Star…he took out a target at a thousand yards while under fire. Ended up leading his platoon out of some desert hellhole with three injured. And one of those three was him."

Her breath caught. "He was wounded?" But he had seemed fine, strong, and there had been no sign…

Shane nodded. "But nobody knew it, apparently, until he got everybody back safely. He even carried one of them half the time." He smiled slowly. "I think he found the brothers he should have had, there."

"Is he…out? Because he was hurt?"

"He's out, but I don't know if that's why. He took that part out of what he showed me." His mouth twisted slightly.

"That hasn't changed, it seems. He doesn't want anyone feeling sorry for him."

"He never did." It came out barely above a whisper.

"I talked to Judge Morales yesterday afternoon, and he made a call. Talked to one of his final training officers, who told him in his experience, guys who come in like Scott did usually go one way or the other. They either continue their old habits and become a problem to be shed as soon as possible, or...they change entirely and excel. He said Scott was the best example of the latter he'd seen in a very long time."

And suddenly nothing else mattered except that she'd been right about him. "I knew he could do it. I just knew it," she whispered.

"I know you did. And that he came back to show the judge he hadn't wasted the chance he gave him says a lot, too."

"What about Pete's funeral?" she asked, curious about what he'd say.

"I think that was why he came now, and not his main reason. Why would it be, after how he grew up?"

They don't want me, Sage. They never did. They tried to give me away, as soon as they got the test results that said I wasn't a match for Pete.

Scott, no—

I found the paperwork. To give me up for adoption.

She shook off the memory of the day she'd first realized the size of the betrayal he was dealing with. She gave her brother a sideways look. "You weren't nearly as positive about him back then. I seem to remember you telling me to stay away from him, and vice versa."

Shane only shrugged. "He wasn't the man he clearly is now, back then."

She studied the man who had held their family together in the wake of disaster. He lowered his own coffee mug and gave her a questioning look. "In a way, he became the personification of the most important Shane-ism, didn't he?"

He blinked. "What?"

She said it softly, and let all the love she felt for her big brother into her voice. "That sometimes all you can do is start where you stand."

He looked startled, then lowered his gaze as if she'd embarrassed him.

But he was smiling.

After he'd gone Sage sat for a while, her coffee cooling unnoticed as she was focused inward. She kept batting away one persistent gnat of a thought, with the logical reasons that it was pointless, too much time had passed, it was useless, and would be fruitless. And yet it kept flitting back, no matter how many times she brushed it off. Finally, realizing it was not going to leave her alone, she rose from the table, emptied her mug and put it in the dishwasher, and by force of habit set up the coffeemaker for a fresh pot for anyone who wandered in and needed it. Then she walked over to the rack on the wall, grabbed her denim jacket and her keys, and headed for her truck.

HE HADN'T MEANT to come here. Hadn't even really been aware of doing it; he'd only been driving around, looking, seeing how things had changed and not changed. There were some buildings, mostly residential, where there hadn't been, and a couple of new commercial areas. Last Stand was doing all right, it seemed. Growing. He couldn't quite quash a grin as he wondered how much of that might have to do with the reputation of their police chief, now that he was an unwitting and—Scott was certain—unwilling Internet star.

He slowed as the road began the familiar curve. Was startled to see the sign at the head of the long, winding driveway that snaked toward the trees that flourished at the edge of the creek. The Hickory Creek Inn, Bed and Breakfast? The Buckley place was a B and B now?

He couldn't see the big house from here. And he suppressed the urge to park and take the old route he'd always taken, climbing the fence and sneaking down to the bend in the creek, to their spot. He didn't want to even think about the look on Chief Highwater's face if he was to get caught and turned in. And he grimaced at the memory of the stupid kid he'd been, trespassing on property owned by a Texas Ranger, even a retired one. Because he knew damned well the philosophy of once a Marine, always a Marine, had probably been invented by the Rangers.

But maybe he didn't own it anymore, maybe he'd sold it to whoever turned it into an inn. That was hard to comprehend; he'd always had the thought that the Buckleys would forever be part of Last Stand, as much as the Highwaters, the Corbyns, the McBrides, or even Minna Herdmann, the matriarch who had been beyond old when he'd left ten years ago.

He made the turn, driving slowly as he tried to think of how to explain why he was here, why he wanted to…just look. Surely people must do that sometimes, look around a place, perhaps before they decided to book a room?

He parked at the far end of the allotted guest parking area. There didn't seem to be anyone around this Friday morning, outside the main house anyway. Maybe the weekenders hadn't arrived yet. He hesitated, then laughed at himself. He'd crept solo into enemy territory with less trepidation than this. He got out of the car and headed toward the trees along the bank of the creek. When he reached the edge of the grove he saw a sign pointing out several walks, obviously for guests. One of them was described as "Creek Overlook," and he felt an odd qualm. There was only one place along here that could be.

Their place.

He shouldn't be surprised. Ten years was a long time, and this place was no longer just a large private home. He quashed his regret, something he'd learned a lot about in those ten years. And he started down the path indicated. He'd never come at it from here, so he scanned the area; it was second nature now. But then, he'd always been careful creeping through the trees from the other side, too. In fact, it had been a sort of lighter version of his last ten years, sneaking, skulking to a desired position, and hoping the enemy— in this case Ranger Buckley—didn't spot him.

That sixth sense he'd developed was tingling when he

reached the point where he could see the pecan tree that had shaded their spot. Not in the Sage-is-already-here way he used to feel, but in warning. Someone else was. The teenager buried inside him jolted to alertness, yelling at him to run, get away. With a rueful shake of his head he kept going.

He recognized the man sitting on the limestone ledge reeling in a fishing line immediately, mainly because ten years had made little difference in him. He mentally reassessed his guess as to Texas Ranger Frank Buckley's age. Back then he'd been woefully unaware of anyone's misery except his own, but he did remember something about the man being injured in the line of duty. Maybe he'd been forced to retire from active duty medically, not because he'd hit retirement age. Maybe he hadn't been as old as Scott had thought.

Which made the fact that the guy hadn't caught him back then even more amazing.

Buckley stood up. He looked sound enough, moved well enough. Scott noticed some gray at his temples, but otherwise his hair was as dark as it had ever been. There were more lines on his face, but those eyes were as clear and sharp as ever. He remembered running into the man, almost literally, in town one day, and had stared into those dark eyes, wondering if he could read minds with that piercing gaze.

"Well," Buckley drawled, "been wondering if you'd show up."

Scott blinked. "You have?"

"What I'd do, coming home for the first time in a decade. Visit all the old spots. As you can see, things have changed a bit."

The old spots... "You...knew?" First the priest, and now this?

"That you hung out here? Of course I did. Did you know this was my place?" Scott nodded, feeling a little stunned. "Then you were either gutsier or stupider than I thought."

Scott swallowed. "I'd go with stupid. I figured because you hadn't caught me—I thought—I was too clever for you."

"Did you."

It wasn't spoken as a question, and Scott couldn't read the man's expression. "It was...who I was then. No respect for others' rights."

Something changed in Buckley's gaze. "Or no respect for yourself?" he asked, his voice unexpectedly soft.

Scott looked away, taken aback by the astute observation. He stared at the creek, where the water was running high and the bend looked deep enough to actually swim in. Coming back here—contrary to what Buckley had said, he didn't think of it as home—was still stirring things up he'd rather have kept undisturbed, but this was not a front he'd expected at all. The judge, the Highwaters—Sage—and now this man?

"You have the look now of a man who knows his own worth," Buckley said.

Scott looked back at him then. "Yes, sir," he said. And something, some level of understanding made him ask,

"Why didn't you ever turn me in?"

"You weren't doing any harm, that I could see." The Ranger's mouth quirked. "And believe me, I checked. If there had been any sign of drug paraphernalia, it would have been a different story."

Scott gave him a wry smile. "You didn't find the beer bottles."

"No. But I figured if you were sober enough to remember to police your ground, I wasn't going to come down on you for that."

"So you knew that, too?"

"I did. And"—the man's gaze narrowed—"I checked for condoms after the Highwater girl started joining you."

Scott felt a chill followed by a rush of embarrassed heat. "We never—I didn't—" He floundered, stopped, then said quietly, "I wouldn't. Even like I was then, I wouldn't. She deserved better."

For a long moment Buckley said nothing. Then, in that same soft tone he'd used before, but this time tinged with unmistakable respect, he said, "Welcome home."

Coming from this man, in this tone, gave Scott the same sort of feeling as having that Bronze Star pinned on him, for that last mission. As if he'd proved his worth.

"And now," Buckley said, picking up his fishing pole in the same instant Scott felt that tickle at the back of his neck, "I'll leave you two to…revisit this place."

And Scott knew before he turned around that it was Sage.

Chapter Nine

Ranger Buckley reached her a few yards before the lookout.

He paused, smiling at her. "He's become quite a man. But I suspect you knew he could and would, given the chance."

She'd always liked Frank Buckley, knew her brothers all liked him, and not only because they, as most Texans did, had a very healthy respect and admiration for the Rangers. She knew he'd retired on a medical, after a bullet had shattered his shooting hand. But it hadn't affected his mind or his twenty-plus years of knowledge, and more than once Shane or Sean had come to him for advice, or to bat around a case they were wrestling with.

But right now she wanted to toss the respect and hug the man for what he'd said. And she wasn't sure what that said about her own emotional state. But she answered him with the truth.

"Yes," she said, her throat tight. "I did."

The tall, lean man merely nodded. "I wish you luck, then."

He started toward the inn, leaving her on the path wondering what would constitute luck for her just now. She wasn't sure encountering Scott here qualified, for several reasons. Although it did hint that while he'd clearly changed a great deal, at the core he was still the boy she'd loved. So maybe she should have known he would be here.

He hadn't turned around, although he had to know she was here. She'd seen Ranger Buckley speak to him after he'd spotted her coming. And it was confirmed when she got close enough and he said, still without looking at her, "He knew. He knew all along we were coming here."

"Can't say I'm surprised. We were silly to think we could put one over on a Texas Ranger."

"But he let us keep coming." He gave a slow shake of his head. "I used to hate knowing people felt sorry for my family. But now I realize that that's probably the only reason I didn't get tossed in juvie three or four times. Even Mr. Diaz didn't press charges when I broke that cage open."

"Of course he didn't, because you did it to help that chick who'd gotten caught in the wire."

"He still could have. He's not exactly the most forgiving guy."

"Well, if that's why he didn't, then something good for you came out of all the ugly."

He grimaced. Lapsed into silence for a long moment. Then, with another visible breath, he nodded toward the spot between the rocks that had drawn them both here.

"It's long gone."

She swallowed. "I knew it would be. They don't call us Flash Flood Alley for nothing."

"The escarpment and the terrain and the orographic effect."

She blinked, startled even out of the emotions trying to rise within her. She knew he had to mean the Balcones Escarpment, the ridge that ran practically from Del Rio to Dallas and that the Hill Country sat upon, but she had no idea what the other thing meant. "The what effect?"

"When wind carrying a lot of moisture hits a geographical feature that pushes it up, which makes it cool, and it releases the moisture as rain."

He still wasn't looking at her, which was probably a good thing since she was staring at him. "They teach you that in sniper school?"

If she'd startled him with that knowledge, it didn't show. She had the feeling it would take a lot more to startle him these days. Wondered if all the control he'd had to exert as a kid, to keep from spinning apart, had helped him become what Shane had told her he'd become. And when he spoke, it was as if the question had been genuine instead of a prod.

"They do teach us about weather, since it can affect a shot. But actually, Mrs. Valencia did."

Sage didn't know what stunned her more, finding out he'd actually paid attention in at least one class—although it was hard not to in the legendary Mrs. Valencia's class—or that he'd remembered. Not to mention the new connection that made this somehow more…personal.

"She taught history."

"I think she figured that was part of history. Why the Hill Country is the Hill Country." Finally he turned to look at her. And he was frowning. "Taught? She didn't die, did she?"

"No," Sage said quickly. "She retired."

"I always figured she was too tough to die. But I also thought she'd be teaching until she did."

Sage couldn't help smiling at that assessment, because had circumstances been different she thought he'd likely have been right. "She retired six years ago to help with her grandson when his father was killed…in action."

Her smile had vanished the instant she realized exactly what she was saying and to who. To who he was now anyway. And the shadow that darkened his gaze now was a new one, one built no doubt by brothers in uniform he'd lost. But all he said was, "I remember her having a grandkid right before…I left." His brow furrowed. "Her daughter's Elena, right?"

Sage nodded. Then grinned, because she couldn't help it. "And as of Christmas, my brother Sean's significant other."

That made him blink. "Whoa."

"Yeah. But it's perfect. He's been mooning over her for years."

Somehow speaking of that relieved some of her tension, probably because her delight for her brother was so cheering. But then he brought it back by glancing again at the spot they had both come to check, taking a deep breath and saying quietly, "I wanted to be sure."

And I'm here because I had to be sure.

She knew it would have nagged at her endlessly if she hadn't. Even knowing it was impossible, given there had been several instances of Hickory Creek overreaching its banks, even cresting above this overlook. Hurricane Harvey among others, although they'd escaped the devastation that had hit the coast.

He looked back at her then, his expression unreadable as he said, "I did write you. But I understand why you don't believe me. I was…kind of crazy back then."

"With reason," she said, feeling a harsh ache building inside her. Here, in this place where they'd spent so many hours, where she'd known even then that he shared this pain with no one else, it seemed as close as if they'd been catapulted back to that time. "And I didn't say I didn't believe you."

"Just that I lied to you before."

She tried to think of a way to explain, how it had hurt when he would deny to her—to *her*—that he was in pain when she knew he was. She couldn't, at the moment. She hadn't expected to run into him here, and she certainly hadn't expected to get into a long conversation with him. The way they used to be, here, in this spot.

As if he were suddenly weary, he sat down on the ledge, not quite where they used to sit but close. He glanced at the swirling creek. And his quiet words told her he was feeling the same way, as if the ten years since then had vanished. "Maybe I should be glad they just didn't drown me, like the runt of a show dog litter." At those words the ache inside her became sharper, deeper. He went on as if merely musing aloud. "I used to wonder if Robbie hadn't been a match for Pete, they would have just kept having kids until one was."

She dropped down to sit as well, but closer to their spot.

A safe yard away. "I guess the Savior Sibling thing wasn't an option yet?"

"Not when he was diagnosed." He glanced at her, his expression wry. "But I heard someone mention that to them once, later. They said they wouldn't have done it if it had been, because it went against their beliefs."

Sage gaped at him. "That goes against their beliefs, but totally abandoning a kid they already had didn't?"

He shrugged again, this time in that weary sort of way she remembered all too well. "They were consumed with saving Pete."

Anger sparked in her, again as if it were those long ago days. "You want to know what I think of Peter Parrish? I think he proves cancer is undiscriminating, because even jerks get it. And that getting it doesn't automatically make you a saint. I don't care if it's not proper to speak ill of the dead, I despise him. He was spoiled rotten, and knowing your parents probably was well before he got sick. And now, all the sacrifices made for him, and he throws it away. Stupidly, in an utterly avoidable way."

Something flared in his green eyes. As if her anger had reached him, had made him…she wasn't sure what.

"I used to wonder, if he'd died back then, if they might notice me. How's that for self-pity?"

"That wasn't self-pity, that was trying to survive. I don't know why you even came home for the funeral."

"Home? Not even. And I'll be out of here as soon as I can." He said it so fiercely she couldn't doubt it. He would be gone again as fast as he could manage it. The home that was precious to her was torture to him. She watched as one corner of his mouth twisted. "I wouldn't have come even for the funeral, if I didn't have other reasons. He wouldn't have come to mine."

Her breath caught, both at the look in his eyes and the tone of his voice. "I would have," she said tightly. "I would have cried. For the rest of my life, every time I thought of you I would have cried." She didn't mention how often she'd done so anyway.

He was staring at her. And then he said something that sent her even deeper back into those days when her moments with him were what kept her going after her father's death. "What happened to cowgirls don't cry?"

"Some things are too big for cute sayings."

A long silent moment passed before he said, "Speaking of cowgirls, why aren't you a cop? Don't tell me your brother really meant it?"

"That if he was chief by then he wouldn't hire me? He only said that as a challenge. I finally realized he wanted me to be sure it was what I wanted, not just all I knew. And he was right. I got through the academy, proved I could do it, then changed my mind. Realized I didn't really want to do it. So now I run the ranch, handle the horses. Does it matter?"

"I just…I always thought of you that way. That by now you'd be halfway to being the next Chief Highwater."

"You couldn't have thought much, or you would have at least written or emailed me. I understand they do have computers in the military." It came out more sourly than she'd intended, but it was how she felt so she didn't apologize. She saw his jaw tighten.

And then he turned his head to look at her and his eyes, those brilliant green eyes, were more intense than she'd ever seen them. "That's one of the things I put in that letter. I had to put it all behind me, Sage. Can you understand that? That if I hadn't cut myself loose completely, if I'd tried to hang on to even you, I would have gone under?"

She felt a jab of something she couldn't name, somewhere between pain at the remembered desperation in his tone and warmth at the way he'd said "even you." It made her say, quietly, "That's part of the reason I changed my mind about being a cop. I didn't ever want to have to arrest a kid like you'd been. Trapped. Caught." She thought of what Shane had told her, what the man who had trained Scott had said. "And then you turned it around. You grabbed the one chance you had and you excelled."

Something changed in his gaze then, as if her words had registered, had mattered.

"It took everything I had, and sometimes I felt like I was bleeding to death from a thousand cuts. But I didn't care, because it kept me from thinking about the biggest thing, the gaping hole. You."

He was getting to her, just as he always had. Because they were talking, as they always had. In this moment it was as if the ten intervening years had vanished. Yet she knew it was impossible to go backward, and tried to focus. She'd known back then that he told her things he told no one else, and that trust had meant the world to her. It had been the most precious thing left to her, after losing both her father and the brother she'd been closest to.

It made her blurt out now, "I spent a long time wishing we'd…gone ahead back then. That I'd forced the issue. That I'd stood up to my brothers when…you wanted me."

He went very still. She saw him swallow, hard, as if his throat was suddenly tight. "No," he said hoarsely. "I would have ruined your life, then."

And it was all she could do not to ask, "And now?" But she did not, because he'd already made the bottom line clear. Last Stand was still and would ever be a painful memory for him. Not his home.

And for her, no place else ever would be.

Chapter Ten

SCOTT HAD NEVER been so thankful to hear his cell phone chime an incoming text. Even when he saw it was from Robbie, asking if he was going to show up at the family meeting to finalize the details of the funeral tomorrow. He must have grimaced, because Sage asked, "Problem?"

"Just Robbie, about a family meeting this afternoon."

"So you're suddenly a part of the family? All those years of being the one left out, now they want you around?"

His gaze shot to her face. "Apparently so."

"Tell me you're not going to this…meeting?"

"No. Going to the funeral is all I can handle."

She nodded, as if she understood perfectly. But then, she always had. "Had any good Tex-Mex since you've been back?"

He blinked. "Uh…no."

"Valencia's makes some wicked good huevos rancheros for breakfast, and I'm starved. I kind of forgot to eat."

His mouth quirked upward at one corner. "So did I."

"Then let's go." She stood up.

Go. Together. Publicly. "You sure you want to do that?"

"I'm sure I'm hungry," she said with a shrug. "So are

you."

That was so Sage he couldn't help smiling. Her eyes widened, and he realized it was probably the first time he'd truly smiled at her since he'd set foot back in Last Stand.

They ended up having to park some distance apart, Scott taking a spot very close to where he'd first parked, in front of the church. He saw the door he'd opened for Father Nunes standing ajar, heard some rather complex whistling coming from inside. He stuck his head in, caught the strong whiff of paint.

"How's it going?" he called out.

The man turned around, pulled the paint mask he had on down, and smiled. "Slowly. How's the return home going?"

"About like I expected," Scott said. "Better in some ways."

"That's good to hear."

Scott looked around the big room. Father Nunes was the only occupant. "You doing all this on your own?"

"Keeps me out of trouble."

Scott laughed. "I'd think you'd get some volunteers."

"You offering? Because you, I think I'd take. As opposed to some of my willing but inept flock."

"I would, if I was sticking around." He found, a little to his surprise, he meant it. He liked the guy, and a bit of physical labor sounded appealing right now, with all this mental turmoil foaming around him.

"If you change your plans, I can pretty much guarantee I'll be here," the man said, with a gesture at the sizeable room.

He walked toward Valencia's pondering yet another compliment, here in this place he would have expected the opposite everywhere. *You, I think I'd take.*

Of course, Father Nunes didn't know his history. Well, obviously other than the hiding in the church courtyard. Or maybe he did. He'd never really thought about the possibility that he might still be a topic of conversation in Last Stand years after he'd gone. He'd always figured he'd be forgotten as soon as he was out of sight. A few good riddances and that would be the end of Scott Parrish's story in Last Stand.

But maybe not.

Whatever happened to that Parrish boy, you know, the useless one?

Oh, they dumped him in the military.

Hmpf. They should have dumped him in jail.

He slowed his stride, grimacing as the imagined dialogue played in his head. It had been a long time—a thankfully long time—since that kind of thing had haunted him. He knew how it had started, from comments he'd overheard while sitting in the back of Sergeant Highwater's police car, with a parent using the opportunity to berate her own kid, warning him if he didn't straighten up he was going to wind up in prison just like Scott Parrish. Then there was Mrs. Murray, isolating him from the rest of the class in the "troublemakers' corner," announcing to the others a list of his sins.

For a while after that such exchanges had played through his mind until he wasn't sure which ones he'd heard and which ones he'd made up.

Until Sage had chided him out of it. She always seemed to know when he was veering down that path, and did her best to break him of it. And had, for the most part, succeeded. Not that they still hadn't hit now and then, but when they did he always heard her voice, chanting a list of famous success stories, people others had said the same thing about.

She was already there when he reached the restaurant. "Sorry," he said. "I ended up talking to Father Nunes for a minute."

She gave him a surprised look. "You know him? He's only been here a couple of years."

He shrugged. "I met him when I first hit town. Only parking place I could find was in front of the church."

"He's been quite a change from Father Garza, from what I hear."

"I can see that." He hesitated, then added, "He told me Father Garza knew. About me hiding out there, I mean. But that he'd rather I was there than out getting in trouble."

He saw her eyes widen, then grow thoughtful as she processed. "You know, Parrish, between my brother, Judge Morales, Ranger Buckley, Mr. Diaz, and now Father Garza, it seems you weren't quite as successful getting everybody in town to give up on you as you thought."

He couldn't help it, he gave her a rather sheepish smile. But it wasn't until he reached to pull the door of Valencia's open that what some part of his memory had been trying to shove into his mind registered.

Self-absorbed much?

"Are you sure you want to eat…here?"

She frowned. "I love their food."

"I know, it always was the best in town. But with what happened, right here…"

A shadow flickered across her face, but it didn't linger. "I know. But for me it's not like it was for Sean. I never saw the scene, not like he did." Scott had forgotten that until this moment, that her brother had arrived just after the accident, and had seen the gruesome aftermath. And then, unexpectedly, Sage was smiling again. "But he got over it. For Elena."

Sage was greeted effusively by a woman with a name tag reading Rosalina, who immediately offered to go get Elena for her. Sage laughed and said they were really just here for a late breakfast, and introduced him. If his name registered it didn't show.

"Do you wish the family table?" Rosalina asked.

"No, out here is fine, although thank you for the offer."

"Family table?" Scott asked when they were seated in one of the booths with comfortable brown leather seats. He'd only been in here once, as a kid on a school trip for some cultural thing, but it looked much the same with an adobe fireplace in one corner, brightly colored sombreros on the wall, and big, round gold and black circles that looked like some Aztec artifact above them.

"They have a separate dining room in the back, for private and family functions." She smiled in obvious satisfaction. "And now that includes us, because of Elena and Sean."

"Nice." He lowered his gaze to the place setting of silverware, wondering what it must be like to be part of a family like that. Or for that matter, a family like the Highwaters, tightly bound together even through tragedy.

"Elena's from the Valencia Tile branch of the family," Sage said, gesturing at the colorful tiles that adorned the wall above their table.

He glanced up. He did remember those tiles, remembered liking the intricate pattern and the bright colors. That was about all he recalled about the place, because he'd gotten himself in trouble shortly after they'd arrived by trying to climb the fireplace.

He went back to fiddling with the fork for a moment before he said, without looking at her, "I owe you another apology. I never really put together the magnitude of your losses, I was so wrapped up in my own misery back then."

"You ask me, you still are," she said, and his gaze shot to her face.

"I put it all behind me. Or at least, I thought I had, until I came back here." His mouth twisted wryly.

"Obviously you only walled it off. I think you need to clear the room and blow it up."

A split second passed before a sharp laugh burst from him. Then he was grinning at her. "Not a bad idea." Letting his amazement at her show, he asked, "How are you not bitter? You lost your mother and your father, in such ugly ways."

"I did, but they were...the ways of life. They happen all the time. Besides, I had my brothers. They wouldn't let me." She held his gaze. "It was your loss that was abnormal.

Although you never really had them to lose."

He let out a sour chuckle at that. Ran his thumb over the knife of the setting, over the cutting edge, testing it. A waiter arrived to deposit the requisite chips, salsa, queso, and guacamole, and to take their order. Her suggestion had sounded good, so he let Sage order for them both. She did—extra queso, he noted—and the young man left. And after a moment Sage spoke again.

"You know, if you're still bitter, and if you stay that way, you're letting them win."

"Actually, until I came back, I hadn't thought much about them in a long time."

"Good. They don't deserve a moment from you."

She grabbed a chip and scooped up some of the thick queso. He watched her savor it, until he realized he was getting too into watching the way her mouth moved and the look of pleasure on her face. He grabbed a chip of his own and focused on a scoop of guacamole, denying it was because sharing the queso in this moment would be too…something.

"They were in a tough place," he said after he swallowed the crisp chip adorned with the luscious dip.

Her brows rose. "Making excuses for them now?"

"Let's just say I have more perspective now than I did then. I don't hate them, I just…don't care."

They both kept eating in between talking. "But you're here," she said.

"I told you, I had other reasons. The funeral is just why I came now."

"Thanking Judge Morales."

"Which mushroomed into thanking not only him, but also your brother." He took in a deep breath. "And most of all, you."

"I knew what I knew about you, and what you could be if you were given half a chance." Her voice went so soft it sent a shiver down his spine. "And you proved me right."

It took him a moment, to be sure his voice would be steady, to answer her. "I couldn't let you down. You had faith in me when no one else did."

"I think you've found out that's not completely true."

He shook his head. "They wouldn't have, if not for you."

"Then tell me something. Why did it make you so mad when I thanked you for your service?"

"Don't thank me," he said. "Thank the ones who didn't come back. They're the ones who really paid the price."

"I do thank them. Often," she said. "But that doesn't really answer my question."

He sighed. "It wasn't what you said. It was…that you were the one who said it."

"Me?" She sounded startled.

"I get it, appreciate it. But that's what…strangers say, when you're in uniform."

"Oh." She studied her own silverware for a moment, then looked back at him with those blue eyes he'd never gotten out of his mind. "What was I supposed to say?"

I'm glad you're here.

I missed you.

I love you.

He jerked his gaze away, afraid what he'd thought might

show. This wasn't supposed to happen. None of this was. For a guy who'd thought he'd left Last Stand and everything in it far, far behind, he wasn't doing too well.

He'd never been so glad to see a plate of food arrive.

Chapter Eleven

Sage had been hungry enough that she let his non-answer—unless that moment when some sort of fierce emotion had seemed to flash in those green eyes of his was an answer—slide while they ate. What talk there was, was mostly about the food, which they'd nearly finished when Elena came out to say hello. She introduced them.

"My mother remembers you," Elena said.

Scott gave a short, wry laugh. "I'm sure she does. She sent me to detention often enough."

He hadn't winced at the knowledge, Sage noted. As if he'd resigned himself to being a topic of discussion once the family name was back on the Last Stand grapevine with Pete's death.

"Actually, she said you were whip-smart but out of control. She and Shane had a discussion about you before you went before Judge Morales, and I suspect she called the judge. He's a distant cousin of hers."

Sage was sure her own surprise at this, which she'd had no idea about, was nothing compared to his. He managed a creditable conversation for another minute or so, but after Elena had gone he lapsed back into total silence. She let it spin out for a few moments before she said quietly, "More proof you weren't quite the write-off you always thought you were."

"I don't understand," he admitted, fiddling with the knife that lay across his now empty plate. "I figured I'd need to apologize to everybody in town who knew me then."

She smiled. "If that's how you felt, then you have truly come a long way. The boy I knew was so busy trying to survive he didn't have anything left to think about other people."

"Except you," he said, then looked as if he wished he hadn't said it.

She wanted to ask, to push, but the restaurant had filled up with the regular lunch crowd by now, and it didn't seem the place for a private conversation. Maybe she should have said yes to the family dining room, although the two of them at a table that would seat at least a dozen seemed rather lonely.

Not nearly as lonely as leaving everything and everyone you've ever known behind, like he had to.

She was feeling a little off balance. She'd gone through so many stages after he'd left. It had taken her best friend, Jessie McBride, to point it out to her, that she was going through grief all over again, losing Scott only two years after losing her father and, in essence, a brother. But it made sense. She'd been so sad he was gone, yet glad his suffering here was over, but at the same time furiously angry that he'd gone without a word to her, when she'd thought she mattered to him.

Except he hadn't gone without a word.

She waited until they were done and outside. "Tell me what the letter said."

He closed his eyes for a moment. And said softly, "Everything I didn't have the nerve to say to your face."

"Like?" She needed to hear it. Needed to know what seventeen-year-old Scott had thought, felt, wanted to tell her.

He opened his eyes. Let out an audible breath. "Walk with me? This could take a while." She nodded, and they headed for Main Street. They were in front of the pet store on the corner before he spoke again. "You saved my sanity, Sage. Maybe even my life, because without you I'm not sure I would have made it."

"All I did was talk to my brother."

"I didn't mean that. I meant everything. All the times you were the only one who noticed I was alive, except for when…"

"When you got in trouble?" He nodded. "I knew, you know. I knew why you seemed to work at getting into trouble. It was the only time they even looked at you, wasn't it?"

His mouth curved into a wry smile. "Before I finally realized I was happier when they just ignored me. But the only reason I got to that point at all was you. If I hadn't had you…I don't think I would have made it."

Her chest was so tight she could barely speak. "I know you were…teetering. I could feel it. A couple of times I was so scared for you."

"I knew that. And that's what I meant. When I didn't take that dive, it wasn't because I found the courage to go on, it was because I couldn't do that to you. Not after your father."

She halted. Was vaguely aware of the colorful display in the flower shop window, but her focus was on him. "It would have destroyed me then."

"And that's what kept me going." He reached out and gently brushed a finger over her cheek. "Sometimes it scared me, how much I needed you."

The contact made her shiver. She had to make a conscious effort to focus on what he was saying. "That's when you tried to pull away, isn't it? When you wouldn't show up at the creek for a couple of days?"

He nodded. "But I had to come back. Or I would have ended it. The longer I stayed away from you, the more it built. I meant what I said, Sage. You saved me." He let out a deep breath. "And that's what I tried to say in the letter."

"Scott, I—"

"Excuse me, Miss Highwater."

Sage jerked back to her surroundings, and saw she was in the way of the doorway to the flower shop, blocking the rather imperious man who'd spoken. She instinctively stepped aside, a "Sorry" on her lips before she realized who it was.

Peter Parrish Sr.

Scott's father.

Scott's father, who had glanced at the man beside her and registered…nothing. And then gone inside the shop without a backward look.

The man hadn't even recognized his own son.

The chill that had overtaken him at the sight of his father faded. He'd thought himself prepared for the chance he might run into him or his mother before the funeral, but apparently he hadn't been. Or this time spent with Sage had softened him up too much, and he'd let his guard down.

"I cannot believe that man!"

His gaze shot back to her face. And he realized she was furious. Something temptingly soft and warm expanded inside him. As if he were that kid again, watching her get angry on his behalf. As no one else ever had.

But then she turned back to him, her gaze narrowing in that way that had always meant her agile mind was racing. "You haven't seen him since you got here."

He only shrugged, since he didn't want to snap out, "What did you expect?"

"Have you even seen your brother?"

"No. We've talked, and texted, but not met in person."

"So you've had no contact with anyone in your family at all?"

"And we're all better off for it. They never have and never will forgive me for all the trouble I made when I was here. I'm sure they were glad to be rid of me."

"Then why were they were so angry when you left—"

She stopped. He stared at her. "What? Why would they give a damn? I figured they'd be glad to be rid of me."

He could almost hear her mind racing now. "Maybe they just missed their whipping boy."

"Now that, I'd believe."

"You sure you don't want to make that family meeting? Maybe armed?"

In an instant his mood shifted, and he burst out laughing. She'd always been able to do that for him. And it was all he could manage not to pull her into a fierce hug, right here on Main Street.

"I don't dare. I feel too much like shooting something."

She looked suddenly thoughtful. "We can arrange that, you know."

"What?"

"We have a shooting range now."

We. Possessive. Because Sage Highwater was ever and would always be of Last Stand. *Unlike you, who can't wait to get the hell out of here and away from…everything.* Except for her.

"You do?" he finally got out.

She nodded. "Lock and Load. Out by the cemetery."

He kept a straight face. "Good choice of neighbors for a range."

"Exactly. They don't complain much."

And then they both laughed and started walking again; he had no desire to still be there when his father came out.

"I'd like to see the range, but I didn't bring any weapons."

She gave him an obviously exaggerated goggle-eyed look. "You came to Texas unarmed?" When he laughed she said, "Don't worry, they have plenty you can borrow."

It was a few more steps before he asked, "Whose idea was

the range?"

"Mike Fleming's," she said. She gave him a sideways look. "It won't offend your sensibilities, will it? A Marine, going to a range run by a former Army guy?"

"It might, if I was still active duty."

She stopped walking. "It wasn't medical, was it?"

He shook his head. He still felt a bit conflicted about leaving, but his gut knew it was the right thing. He'd done ten years, proved all he had to prove. And if they really needed him, they could recall him.

But her instant concern sent that soft, warm feeling through him again. "They didn't retire me, if that's what you mean. I was WIA a couple of times, but—"

"I know."

He blinked. Then realized. "Your brother told you."

She nodded. "That's the first time in a while I've seen my brother in awe of someone. Besides Lily, of course."

The thought of Shane Highwater in awe of him was laughable. Yet she'd said it with quiet seriousness. "Lily?"

"Lily Jones. His fiancée."

"Good for him."

She nodded again. "He deserves all the happy life can give a person. He held us all together."

"I owe him for that, too. Holding you together so you could hold me together." His mouth quirked. "Even if he did want you to have nothing to do with me."

"He just didn't want me getting hurt."

"Neither did I. That's why I tried to stay away those times." He gave her a curious look. "I have to admit, I was a little surprised he didn't come after me, once you told me he knew about…us."

"I promised him we weren't having sex."

He almost jerked back, gaping at her. "You what?"

"I told him to back off, because it wasn't like we were having sex or something." She made a wry face at him. "Not for lack of me trying, mind you."

"Believe me, I remember."

And he did. Vividly. As hard as it had been to hold back at seventeen, it hadn't eased much after he'd gone. And as the years went on he'd still sometimes awakened after dreams of her, dreams that had grown in eroticism the more he'd learned about what would have happened had he given in to her coaxing as a teenager. And none of his experiences since then had come close to his imaginings. Because no woman had ever gotten to him the way young, innocent, and stubborn Sage Highwater had.

"Scott!"

The shout snapped him out of a physical reaction he'd hoped he was past. He should have known better. Sage would have a hold on him forever. He was now as certain of that as he was that she could never be part of whatever life he would build now. Because she would never leave Last Stand, and he would never come back.

He turned in the direction of the shout. Saw a guy headed toward them at a rapid clip. And felt another jolt. A different kind this time.

Because at least his little brother recognized him.

Chapter Twelve

"SAGE, HI," ROBBIE Parrish said.

Scott's one-year-younger brother, the one conceived as Scott had been, solely to save Peter Parrish Jr. had been variously tagged in her teenaged mind as the donor, the prisoner, or in her angrier moments the organ farm. She'd never been angry with him, because he'd had no choice. Although she'd wished when Robbie had been old enough he would have stood up for himself. She knew Scott had tried, had stood up for him, but it had only gotten him locked in his room for a week. And Robbie had meekly gone along anyway.

And the scenario had repeated itself more recently when Pete's liver began to fail six years ago, and they'd harvested half of Robbie's to save him yet again.

"Hello, Robbie," she said neutrally. The thin, quiet young man who tended to fade into the background smiled slightly, then he shifted his attention solely to Scott.

"You really came," he said, almost breathless after his rush to get to them. "I was afraid you wouldn't."

"I almost didn't."

"I'm glad you did. Pete would have wanted you here."

"Bullshit." Scott looked like he regretted saying it and gave a sharp shake of his head. "How are you?"

"Awful, of course. I can't believe he's really gone."

Again Sage felt a pang of conscience. Someone had died, after all, someone some people had cared for, whether she understood why or not. It didn't seem right to be…not glad about it, but feel that it was no great loss.

It was a moment before Scott said, so neutrally she knew it was intentional, "I'm sorry everything you sacrificed was for nothing."

Robbie's brows lowered. "It wasn't for nothing. He got a lot more years."

"What did he do with them?"

Robbie blinked this time. And Sage thought suddenly that he looked much younger than he actually was, which was a year younger than Scott's twenty-seven. And for really the first time she wondered about Scott's mother, and how she must have felt about intentionally getting pregnant again so soon, because the first effort at a spare parts supplier hadn't worked.

"What do you mean?" Robbie asked.

"Those years you gave him, literally with your blood, bone, and body, what did he do with them? Did he accomplish something, have a career, a family?"

Sage could have answered that, for most of those years anyway; if Scott Parrish had been the town bad boy, his brother had become the town cliché. Selfish, entitled, and still living in his parents' house even after years of being recovered and relatively healthy, until he'd finally moved out at twenty-eight. Into an apartment in Marble Falls she suspected his wealthy parents had paid for, although maybe she was misjudging that, maybe he'd finally gotten a job.

Not that it mattered to the perceptions people had of either of them. The big difference she saw was people tolerated Pete's royal attitude, and forgave him because of what he'd been through.

They'd never forgiven Scott, because they'd never known or even thought about what he'd gone through.

"No," Robbie said slowly.

"So, did he maybe help others facing what he faced?" Sage asked, the effort it took to keep her own voice even telling her how hard it had to have been for Scott.

"Oh. No, he didn't like talking about it." He shifted his gaze back to his brother. "You're really not coming to the family meeting?"

"You'll manage without me."

Robbie lowered his gaze, as if his own toes had suddenly become fascinating. "I always envied you, you know."

She felt Scott go very still. "I'm not surprised. They weren't drilling holes or cutting into me."

His brother's head came up sharply. "Not that. I meant…you were free. To go and do…what you wanted. Even be reckless, if you wanted."

"While you had to take care of yourself, not for your own sake, but for his."

Robbie's expression hardened then. "You're glad he's dead, aren't you?"

"No." Scott let out a long breath. "I've seen too much

death to welcome it anywhere. I'm just sorry for what you went through. At least that's over."

Robbie seemed to deflate a little. "Yeah."

"Was he good to you, Robbie?" Sage asked. She had no idea what the family situation after Scott had gone had been, although this was Last Stand and she could have easily found out just by asking Mr. Diaz. But afterward, she'd tried to put all things Parrish out of her head. It seemed with zero success when it came to him, at least, judging by how quickly it had all come rushing back.

"It was okay." Robbie shrugged. "He didn't talk about it much, like I said. And I…didn't see him a lot, after he moved to Marble Falls."

Something occurred to her. "He didn't…have another relapse, did he?"

"No." Robbie sighed. It was a tiny, sad thing. As if he, too, had been searching for something that would make sense of a senseless act. A cell phone chimed. Robbie jumped slightly and looked guilty for an instant. "I'm supposed to be meeting Dad."

"He's in the flower shop," Scott said.

Robbie's eyes widened. "So you've already talked to him? Is that why you're not coming?"

"I saw him. He saw me."

When that was all Scott said, Sage couldn't stop herself. "And he didn't even recognize Scott. Walked right past him."

"Maybe he didn't really see you."

"He saw enough to say hello to me," Sage pointed out.

"Go, Robbie," Scott said. "You don't need him mad at you."

"Yeah, right." Sage watched the boy—because that's what he seemed to her—walk hastily away.

"God, I can't wait to get out of this stinking town," Scott muttered.

That stung, but it was no surprise. She couldn't really blame him, after all. But it helped make her tone beyond sour when she said, "I really, truly regret not telling Shane your mother hit you."

"But you didn't."

She shook her head. "I promised you I wouldn't."

"She never hit Robbie."

"Of course not. She couldn't damage the donor, now could she?" She sighed. Gave him a sideways glance. "Want to go out to Lock and Load with me? Suddenly *I* feel like shooting something."

That earned her enough of a smile that the pressure inside her eased a little. Which was crazy. Because twenty-four hours ago she'd been convinced she didn't care a whit about seeing him, had been happy it would be easy to avoid seeing him at all. But that was when she'd thought he'd left without a word. When instead he'd left her words that twisted her into knots even now. Because what he'd told her he'd written had meant more to her than she would have thought possible, especially after ten years.

And she was beginning to realize Scott Parrish had the same effect on her now that he always had. An effect no one else had ever had. So what did she do about that?

Set myself up to spend half the day with him.

Even knowing he'd hit the road out of Last Stand five minutes after the funeral was over.

THEY TOOK HER car, leaving his parked in front of the church. If it wasn't safe there, he wasn't sure where it would be. But knowing Chief Highwater, he doubted crime ran rampant in his town.

Sage drove with an easy smoothness that didn't surprise him at all. It struck him belatedly they'd probably be going past the cemetery where the funeral would be tomorrow. He wished it was over. Pondered not going, even though he was already here. He'd accomplished his main tasks, the real reasons he'd come back. Maybe he should just leave. It wasn't like his presence was going to do anything except probably start the usual family quarrel.

"If one of my brothers had been sick, I would have done anything to help save him," Sage said abruptly into the silence.

"I know." He paused, wondering if there had been, at last, a criticism in those words. She had never, back then, wavered in her support of both him and how he felt. He himself had been full of enough self-disgust that it had been a glorious relief to have someone who didn't blame him or hate him for how he felt.

"But," she said as she negotiated a turn, "it would have been my choice."

He only realized how he'd tensed up by how he relaxed when she made the point that had always been the crux of it for him. "Yes."

"I can't imagine living knowing you were only alive because they'd needed bits and pieces of you to keep someone else alive." She gave him a quick glance as they made the turn onto the Hickory Creek Spur and headed east. "But knowing they thought you a waste because you couldn't serve that purpose is worse."

They'd had variations on this discussion back then. But he had perspective now he hadn't had then. As he'd told Robbie, he'd seen too much death now to be sanguine about it.

"I think Robbie always thought I was angry because I wasn't a match for Pete. But I never knew he envied me the freedom I had, that he didn't."

"You both paid a price for where you ended up, through no fault of your own."

"I suppose."

She glanced at him again. "If it had been possible…would you have traded with Robbie?"

"If I'd been a match, he wouldn't exist," Scott pointed out.

"I know that. But…who was really better off? Was he the lucky one, or were you?"

"I don't know." His brows lowered slightly. "I never thought about it quite like that."

"I think you both got screwed," she said bluntly. "One of you was needed, one of you not, but neither of you were really loved, not in the way you should have been." She looked suddenly stricken. "And Pete may have been the loved one, but he went through hell, too. So maybe you all got screwed. Maybe it's no wonder he ended up…like he did, doing something so stupid he died young anyway."

He didn't look at her. Wasn't sure he dared just now. This was just so…Sage, fierce in his defense, yet seeing the other side. "You always were far too wise for the kid you were. I never understood why you insisted on hanging out with someone as wackshit as me."

"You know what all the Highwaters stand for, each in their own way?"

He blinked at the apparent non sequitur. "Uh…"

"Justice. Something you never got."

"Until you stepped up for me."

"Shane's the one who talked to—"

"Don't, Sage. Don't belittle what you did." He sucked in a breath. "It must have made it even worse, that after you did that you thought I'd left without even a word."

"Even if you had, you made up for that today," she said softly.

"I should have talked to you, in person. You deserved that, at the very least. But it all happened so fast, and I was afraid the chance would vanish, that they'd change their minds and not take me."

"Because who would ever want scapegrace Scott Parrish?" she said quietly.

He went still. "That's the other thing I need to thank you for. Because I believed that, Sage. That no one would, or could. Then…remember the day you brought me that medal of your grandfather's?"

She nodded. He remembered the day before his hearing before Judge Morales vividly, when she had presented him with the precious memento, and how she'd told him it was only until he'd earned his own medals, which she seemed utterly certain he would. It seemed even more momentous, now that he knew she'd gone to bat for him so fiercely with her brother.

"That was the day I realized you really thought I was worth something. And that if Sage Highwater thought that, I couldn't be completely worthless."

And it had been the determination to prove her right that had driven him every day since.

Chapter Thirteen

THEY WERE NEARING the cemetery when, rather morbidly, something occurred to Sage. "Did you know my father was watching out for you, while he was alive and chief?"

They were at a curve in the road so she couldn't look at him, but she heard him turn. "I figured I was on his radar. He didn't miss much. If there was a problem in Last Stand, he knew about it. Like I'm guessing your brother does now."

"Shane does, yes, but that's not what I meant. I meant he essentially told Shane, and maybe others, to cut you some slack. That with your family situation, it was only natural you'd…act out a little."

She could risk a glance at him now. He was practically gaping at her. "He…what?"

She looked back to the road. "I think that's where my other brothers got the idea that you were trouble, and that I needed protecting from you."

There was a very quiet moment before he asked, "Is that why you…talked to me?"

"There were a lot of reasons I talked to you." *Many of them hormone-driven…*

She slowed as they passed the entrance to the cemetery, a habit she couldn't seem to break. She hadn't been to visit Dad in a while. They all made their individual treks out here on the anniversary of his death in June, but she usually went in between, just to talk to him.

She'd needed someone to talk to, after he'd died and Kane, her usual confidant, had vanished. Someone who was a step back from her personal tragedy. Another reason she'd been so entranced with Scott. Thinking about someone else's terrible situation helped distract her from her own.

"You know who told me I should go ahead and talk to you, before...your father was killed?" he asked rather abruptly. "Told me that you'd listen like no one else, and understand?"

"Jessie?" she guessed, although she somehow doubted it. Her best friend had agreed Scott Parrish was hot, but had also warned Sage he was one messed-up guy.

Then Scott blasted her equilibrium, already shaken since he'd come home, to bits. "Kane."

She nearly drove off the road. She did pull over, so she could stare at him.

Kane. The sound of him speaking the name she'd just thought echoed in her head. Her brothers had gotten much better since Joey, bless her, had told them they weren't protecting her as they'd thought but hurting her by avoiding even saying his name. Their apparent refusal to even acknowledge he'd existed at all had been a razor's edge slicing deep into a heart already bleeding.

"Explain, please," she said.

"We both got in trouble at school on the same day. Ended up in the waiting room at the principal's office. I knew who he was."

"Of course." She grimaced. "The curse of being a Highwater, everybody in Last Stand knows you."

He shook his head. "I meant...I knew he was your brother. And he knew I...damn, this sounds stalkerish...I'd been watching you."

She was the one gaping now. "What?"

"You were hard not to notice." He shrugged. "You were almost as beautiful then as you are now."

He said it so offhandedly, as if it were a given, as if he was saying the sky was blue. She thought that made it one of the most genuine—and precious—compliments she'd ever gotten. "Go on," she managed to get out.

Again the shrug. "Turned out he knew about me, too, even though he was a year older." She regained a bit of her composure when he perfectly mimicked her own grimace as he added, "The curse of being the family the whole town felt sorry for."

"Some would say felt compassion, but never mind that now."

He lowered his gaze. "Anyway, that's when he said...that. About you."

Her emotions were roiling at this discovery of the gift Kane had, even unintentionally, left her. It was all she could do to keep a relatively calm tone when she said, "But you didn't take his suggestion." Because they hadn't met and talked until after her father—and Kane—were gone.

"I almost did. But then Robbie got mono and things got…hellish for a while." He gave her a wry smile. "They were afraid they wouldn't be able to use him anymore if Pete had a relapse right then."

She bit back a retort that would have bordered on malicious. For a long time she'd felt guilty about her emotional reaction to the situation. Pete had, after all, literally faced death, but that hadn't changed him much that she could see. He was still a spoiled, entitled, eldest son of a cold and harsh man. More than once she'd wondered if that man would have fought so hard for that son if he hadn't been his own namesake.

He smiled a bit sadly at her reaction. But it faded when he said, "And then your dad was killed. And Kane was gone. I didn't know what to say, so I never approached you. Then when I went to the creek that day, you showed up." He gave her a sideways look. "I always wondered about that, if you—"

"I followed you." She admitted it shortly, not wanting to get diverted now. "Why," she said carefully, "did you never tell me this?"

"I didn't want to…hurt you. Remind you."

Sage let out an exasperated breath. "Men! Sometimes I think you're all idiots. You and my brothers. Do you really think if you didn't mention him I'd forget? That I've ever forgotten, or ever would?"

"No," he said quietly. "But I didn't want to be the one to bring it all back if you'd managed to put it out of your mind for a while."

As if she could. Maybe he could compartmentalize like

that, maybe all men could, but she couldn't. She shook her head, wondering if she'd ever understand the male mind. Or if they would ever understand the female mind. But then, maybe that was part of the plan; if someone took the time to try to understand the differences, then maybe that was a sign of…something.

She pulled back onto the Spur.

"Are you…happy you didn't become a cop?"

"In the end I realized I couldn't do what I wanted with our horses and be a good cop, too, so I had to decide. The horses won."

"Lucky them."

"Thinking I made a mistake?"

"No. Just surprised. I had it in my head that's where you'd be, whenever I thought about you."

"I didn't think you thought about me at all," she said as she made the turn into the dirt parking area that ran the length of the range.

He waited until they were stopped near the largest building, which looked like a converted small barn, before he said quietly, "I thought about you. A lot. And whenever I was…in a tight spot, when I thought it might be the end…it was you I thought of."

Once again he'd taken her breath away. She stared at him, trying to comprehend being the person someone thought about in those circumstances. The person *he* thought about in those circumstances. Because she knew he was telling the truth. Scott would not lie about something like that, would not make up some pretty story, even if he had always denied he was in as much pain as she knew he was. And she realized she should never have doubted even for that instant that he had in fact written her.

She'd always been a little bit amused at Slater's tactic of leaving Joey notes every day, but he'd sworn it had been what had convinced her to give them a chance. Now she kind of understood, because she felt a tug of loss that she'd never gotten to read what seventeen-year-old Scott had poured out onto those pages.

"I tried not to think about you...being in spots like that. Did it happen often?"

"A time or two." Since he'd just proven he had a typically male mind, she translated that to "several."

"You faced it with more grace than your brother," she said flatly. "And I don't need any details to know that."

"You're awfully certain. I wasn't."

"You're tougher than he was. Sure, his situation was awful, but he had a support system, he had your parents and Robbie, while you had nobody."

"I had you," he said simply.

And again he took the wind out of her. And she had to hammer her leaping pulse down with the memory of what he'd said.

I'll be out of here as soon as they start tossing dirt on the coffin, and it still won't be soon enough.

He hadn't come home, not to stay. He wouldn't be here at all if not for obligations. And if he hadn't become the kind of man who took care of them. The kind of man she'd always known he could be.

She'd wondered on occasion if she'd fallen in love with an idea, a possibility, not the real person. Wondered whether, if he'd stayed, that idea would have eventually been shattered, if he would have let her youthful faith down.

But he hadn't. He hadn't stayed, and he'd made it more than clear he was never coming back, that Last Stand was not—maybe never had been—his home.

And now that she knew he'd become all she'd imagined, she wasn't sure where that left her.

Chapter Fourteen

SCOTT LET OUT a low whistle as he looked at the target she'd summoned back to her with a push of the button. "Last Stand PD missed out when you changed your mind."

"Rattlesnakes are a lot harder to hit than a stationary target."

"I'll bet you'd be hell on wheels on a tactical course."

"Mike has been thinking of adding one," she said as she policed her brass. "He's got the room."

"Why doesn't he?" He didn't move to help her pick up the spent casings. He doubted she'd appreciate it if he did. Some things were simply personal responsibility.

"He's running this place by himself. And as he says, he's no spring foal anymore."

"Still runs a tight ship," Scott said as he glanced around the indoor range. It was small, only three lanes, but had a full gamut of distance choices and lighting. He'd noticed a cleaning station just outside, and a bank of lockers for weapons kept on site. There was a long worktable for servicing, and Sage had said the man did a bit of repair and customization for people when he had the time. Above all the whole place was tidy, clean and bright inside. "How old is he?"

"I'm not sure." She gave him a sideways glance before she stepped up to the table to clean her Sig Sauer P320. "But he was in the first Gulf War."

He only nodded, but it helped him slot the range master into a category. "He's a trusting sort," he said, given the man had thus far been nowhere in sight although the indoor range had been unlocked.

"We're a trustworthy bunch, his regulars. Want to shoot?"

"I'm no great shakes with a pistol." He'd had to accept that early on, but the unexpected skill he'd discovered with a long gun more than made up for it.

"How about the rifle range then?" she said without quibbling.

His mouth went up at one corner. "Not even a jab at me for that?"

"I feel better," she said easily, "now that I've metaphorically vanquished a demon or two. So what do you say?"

"I don't have a weapon," he pointed out.

She grinned at him. "If it shoots, Mike's probably got it here somewhere."

He had his doubts that the man would loan out a valuable rifle to a total stranger, but he followed her anyway as she walked out of the converted barn.

I'd follow her anywhere.

He gave a sharp shake of his head. He had to stop doing that. Although not thinking about following her when he was behind that cute backside was going to take some willpower. Okay, a lot of willpower. He tried to focus on something else, like the rather intricate braid of her dark hair that went down to the middle of her back. But that only got him thinking about what it would feel like loose, and how he'd like to undo that braid and run his fingers through the long strands he was sure would feel like silk.

How he'd like to think about it trailing over him. Preferably when they were both naked.

He suppressed a shiver. When she came to a halt as they reached a long, covered stretch outside that clearly served as a prep area, with all the various pieces of equipment and targets he was familiar with, he was finally able to concentrate on something other than her. He looked out over the range, saw the distance markers going out so far that he couldn't read the next to the last one with the naked eye, and could barely see the last one. If it was the last one. A thousand yards, he guessed. Over half a mile. A nice, long shot for anyone short of long-distance overwatch.

"What's beyond that?" he asked.

"Open range, for another two miles. Somebody nicked a cow once, but not seriously, the round was pretty spent by then. Mike jokes about putting a target at the two-mile mark."

"It's been done," Scott said. He sensed a presence and started to turn in the moment before a deep, rough-edged voice came from behind them.

"Indeed it has, less than a hundred miles from here. Under perfect conditions and custom equipment of course, so it hardly counts."

The moment he met the steady, level gaze of the man he knew he was a kindred spirit. He had the look, of having seen much, done much, and too much of it ugly. He was shorter than Scott, maybe five-ten or eleven, wiry, heavily tanned with salt and pepper hair in a buzz cut.

Sage introduced them, ending with a smiling, "No Army versus Marine arguments, please."

"Well, now there goes half my repertoire," the older man drawled.

"And half my great comebacks," Scott countered.

They both smiled and shook hands.

"You have something he could shoot here, Mike?" Sage asked. The man's gaze turned assessing. Sage noticed, because she said, in a tone he couldn't quite name, "Shane says he's won a zillion competitions and about every rifle marksman medal they award."

Scott flushed. "Jeez, Sage. I'll blow my own horn if I want it blown."

"Which means never," she said without even looking at him. And it hit him suddenly that the note he'd heard in her voice had been…pride. As if she were proud of him. And his gut knotted at even the thought.

"MOS?" Fleming asked.

"Scout Sniper."

"Well, well," Fleming said at the naming of Scott's Military Occupational Specialty. "One of the unique ones."

Scott shrugged. "I wanted to go for Force Recon, but the brass wanted otherwise."

"Apparently they noticed your skills. Rank?"

"Left a sergeant."

"You really did make good, didn't you?"

The approval in the older man's tone made his gut knot tighter. It was only belatedly he realized that here was yet another person, someone he didn't even know, who apparently knew of his past.

"There are no damn secrets in this town, are there?" he muttered.

"What there are, are people who give a damn," Sage retorted.

"Indeed," the range master said. "So, you want to show me how that 'One Shot, One Kill' motto goes?"

Sage hadn't been kidding when she'd said the man had about every long gun there was. Including the M40 he'd trained on and shot for a good portion of his career. He hefted the familiar weapon, aware of Fleming's watchful gaze, but not caring; in this, at least, he knew how good he was. And in this he was able to close everything else off, even Sage, for too often lives had depended on that ability. And more than once his own life had.

He took a moment to study the air, the very slight wafting from the east. The humidity wasn't bad, being February. He kept assessing until he was as sure as he could be without instruments or a good spotter.

It only took two rounds for him to be sure the weapon shot true, with no idiosyncrasies or pulling off center. He put rounds nearly dead center at each successive distance he tried. The last was technically out of range for these rounds, but he was feeling good so gave it a try, compensating for the distance with a slight shift in trajectory.

It wasn't dead center, and it took countable seconds to get there, but it hit.

Fleming let out a low whistle. "They'll be missing you, son."

"It's a good weapon," Scott said neutrally.

"I like a man who doesn't brag," the man said.

"I like a man who doesn't need to," Sage said, and he felt a kick of that emotion again.

"Hold tight a minute." Fleming turned and disappeared into the storage room that sat at one end of the long, narrow, covered area. It was closer to three minutes when he came back, holding with some care a rifle Scott had only seen on display, in parades, or in movies. "Let's see what you can do with this old baby."

"An M1?" he said as he took it—carefully—when Fleming held the Garand out to him. The man nodded. The weapon was polished to a high sheen, both metal and wood, looking fresh from the factory rather than of World War II vintage. But carved into the stock was a rough image of the Lone Star flag, and underneath the letters *L.S. Tx.* "Wow. This looks like a collection piece. You sure you want me to fire it?"

"If you can load it without losing a thumb. I'd like to see it fired by someone who knows what they're doing. My eyes aren't what they used to be. Getting older's hell, son."

"Beats the alternative," Scott said.

"There is that," the Army vet said with a laugh.

It had been a while since he'd seen one of the classic rifles, or fired .30-06, but the cause of Garand Thumb had always stuck in his mind. So after he'd loaded the square clip into the rifle's magazine he held the bolt back for the split second it took to get his thumb free before the bolt automatically snapped forward and the weapon was ready to fire.

Fleming nodded approvingly. "Go ahead and empty it."

It didn't have the range of modern rifles, but in some ways it felt better, more…classic, he guessed, with the warmth of the wood. With even more care than he'd taken before, he lined up the sights and worked his way from marker to marker out to the 500, each round he fired giving the characteristic pinging sound from the en bloc clip, and hitting solid.

When he'd finished and the rifle ejected the clip that had fed it, an odd sensation swept him. It was as if he could almost feel the weight of its storied history. "If there's a rifle that likely saved the world this is probably it," he murmured, barely aware of speaking aloud.

Then he wondered when he'd gotten so fanciful. And answered his own question. *Since you set foot back in Last Stand.*

But when he looked up at the watching range master, he saw understanding in his face. He met the man's gaze steadily. "It still shoots true."

"Good to hear." The man reached out for it.

"I shot it, I'll clean it," Scott said.

Fleming nodded approvingly, but said, "I'll do it." He paused, then said, "It was my father's. It got him through World War II alive."

For a second Scott just gaped at him. "I... You let me shoot..."

He was so stunned he couldn't finish. His gaze went back to the carved flag and letters on the stock.

"That's how I tracked it down," Fleming said. "He told me he'd done that. He didn't go in until July, after D-Day, and it drove him crazy not to be in the initial invasion."

Scott found his voice again. "Probably another reason he survived."

"Probably. But Operation Cobra was fierce enough. And the weather delays made it worse." Fleming gave him a rather crooked smile. "It was rougher than Desert Storm, I'm guessing."

Scott smiled back then. "Heck," he drawled, "Desert Storm you hardly had time to get sand in your boots." The older man laughed. And for a long moment Scott held his gaze, then said quietly. "Thank you. I'm honored."

Fleming nodded, and Scott thought he saw a sheen of moisture in the older man's eyes as he carried the rifle to the cleaning station.

"That was quite something, Sergeant Parrish."

Sage's soft voice almost made him jump. The sound of it made him realize just how long she had been, uncharacteristically, quiet. When he turned around to look at her, he saw the same kind of sheen in her blue eyes. And there was respect, even admiration in her expression.

And that almost made him forget about the ordeal of the funeral he'd be facing tomorrow.

In fact, it almost put him on his knees.

Chapter Fifteen

SAGE HADN'T FELT so tangled up in a long time.

Probably not since she'd made the decision that the horses were her future, not wearing the badge. It had taken her a long time to be at peace with her choice, but within a year she'd known it had been the right one. Of course it helped that her brothers never made her feel as if she'd made the lesser choice. In fact each of them expressed their gratitude, in their own way, telling her that by taking over the ranch operations she had made it possible for them all to stay together as a family, under one roof, as their father had wanted.

She was reasonably certain this current tangle wasn't going to turn out nearly as well.

Watching Scott shoot with such skill and accuracy had warmed her. But watching him handle Mike's precious memento with such care and reverence, and then treat the older man the same way, had stirred up something deep inside her that she couldn't put a name to.

Of course, the most tangled up she'd ever been in her entire life had been over him, so she supposed she shouldn't be surprised.

She stowed her Sig in the case she kept in the door pocket of her truck, vaguely aware of the sound of another vehicle approaching.

"You really are good with that," Scott said.

She shrugged. If it worked for him, why not her?

As the approaching vehicle stopped, she looked up and saw it was a marked Last Stand police unit. After a moment Ry Murdoch got out, in uniform, likely here for his monthly qualification. Sage saw the tall, lean man's glance linger on Scott for a moment, but saw only curiosity in his expression. Given he hadn't grown up here in Last Stand he wouldn't know who Scott was, and while strangers in town weren't at all an oddity, strangers here at the range were a blip on any cop's radar.

"Hey, Icewater," Ry called out, but he kept going toward the indoor range.

She waved back at him. Wondered how long it would take to get back to Sean or even Shane that their sister had been out at the range with a stranger. Of course, either one of them would immediately guess that it hadn't been a stranger.

"Rylan Murdoch," she said to Scott, trying to forestall the question she knew was coming. "He was in my class at the academy."

Scott was staring at her, and she sighed. Inevitably, he said it. "Icewater?"

"It was my nickname at the academy."

He studied her for a moment. "Why?"

She turned to look at him. "Because I was icy, I suppose."

"You?" His almost boggled expression was, in a way, flattering.

"To them," she amended. "And I was proud of that nickname. I worked hard for it."

"Why?" he asked again.

"I got tired of getting hit on because of my brother. Not Ry, he wasn't like that, but others. They knew Shane was headed for chief, and wanted an in with him."

"And they figured hitting on his little sister was the way?" He sounded so incredulous she couldn't help smiling.

"Kind of the opposite of you, who could have had me anytime you wanted, but didn't because of my brothers."

That shut him up. In fact, he looked as if she'd kicked him in the gut and she wished she hadn't said it. He was silent as, back in the truck, she drove sedately out of the range parking area. She decided to try for distraction.

"What was the worst part of what you did in the Marines?"

He started to answer, then stopped. She had the feeling he'd been going to give some routine, brush-off kind of answer, but had changed his mind.

Then he said, "Other than being the vehicle for authorized homicide?"

That made her breath catch. "Necessary," she said after a moment.

"Yes."

"So yes, that aside, what was the worst part?"

"Should I leave out the snakes? Cobras are scary, but I'd

take ten of them over a couple of sneaky, hide-in-your-boots kraits. Or one saw-scaled viper. You so much as look at one of those sideways and they'll hunt you down and kill you. They make Texas rattlers look like a church social."

Sage couldn't decide if he was dodging, or giving her a peek into what life had been like over there. "Yes, please, leave out the snakes."

"Then the worst was the same as the best. Snipers are…isolated. Alone. Even with a spotter you feel alone."

"And you were used to that," she said quietly, realizing that the snake talk hadn't been a dodge, but a working up to sharing this. She should have realized.

"Yeah."

"What was the hardest thing physically? Once you got through training, I mean."

He looked wary, as if he wasn't sure why she was asking all this. But he answered her, which she counted as great progress.

"Honestly? Moving inches at a time for hours. No, actually, it was getting up and trying to run after being proned out waiting for a shot for a couple of days."

Days? Sage stopped at the turn back onto the road, turned her head to look at him. She was probably gaping, but she couldn't help it; the image was so vivid. She tried to imagine the Scott she'd known, fiery and wild, acting with such…patience.

"They really did remake you, didn't they?" she whispered.

"Taught me," he said. "Things I needed to learn."

If she needed any further proof of how Scott Parrish had grown, matured, she had it now. She made the turn onto the road. Silence held until they neared the cemetery again.

"Want to stop?" she asked. She sensed rather than saw his start of surprise, since she was watching a minivan exit the gates.

"Why would I?" There was an undeniable edge in his voice.

"Just thought maybe you'd want to do a little recon. Make sure you have a couple of quick exit paths fixed in your mind."

There was another moment of silence, then she heard him let out a long breath. "Not," he said, more normally now, "a bad idea."

They found the location easily, once Scott remembered the general area where his grandfather was buried. She noticed he paid little attention to the spot itself, already being prepared, but indeed looked around as if he were searching for the best escapes.

She pointed. "Park at the far end of the lot there instead of near the chapel, and you'll be closest to your car when it's over."

He looked that way. Nodded. "Good obs," he said.

"I haven't forgotten everything I learned in the academy," she said. "Would you mind if we walk out that way?" She pointed toward a rise marked with a simple obelisk.

"Your dad?" he asked softly.

She nodded. "I haven't been here since…the anniversary."

"Sure. I'd like to. To...thank him."

She felt it again, that warmth, that deep stirring. And had to again remind herself there was too much water under the bridge, that he'd blown up that bridge anyway, and that he was dead set on leaving Last Stand in his rearview mirror as soon as he possibly could.

A minute later she was kneeling beside the headstone, pressing fingers to her lips, then the name.

"Elena was there that day," she said when she straightened up.

"I remember."

"She tried to save him, but there was no chance." He was looking at her as if he had no idea what to say to that. She hadn't meant this to be awkward, so she went on quickly. "Sean got there right after, when she was still sitting there on the curb, crying. I think he's been in love with her ever since."

"And now they're...together?"

"Very," she said with a smile. She glanced back at the headstone. "We also found out my dad and Elena's mom had...a thing going. They might even have ended up together, if he hadn't been killed."

He stared at her. "Elena's...Mrs. Valencia?"

"Yeah. Scary, huh?"

"Wow."

"Elena gave us a gift, too," she said softly. "She gave us a whole new way to think about his last words."

His brow furrowed. She'd told him the whole story back then, including what her dying father had told the young woman who had held him at the end. "I thought he just said to find you and tell you it wasn't Mr. Goetz's fault?"

"Elena thinks he meant for her to tell us it wasn't Kane's fault, and to find him."

He drew back slightly. "That...changes things a bit."

"Yes. He didn't mean for it to happen," she said fiercely. "I always knew he didn't. There was a scrape on the side of Dad's boot, and I think his foot came down wrong and he lost his balance. If not for that he would never have fallen in front of that truck."

"It really was an accident."

"Yes."

"Judge Morales said you've never stopped looking for him."

"We haven't. And thanks to both Joey and Elena, we're a lot closer. We know where he was four years ago."

"Where?"

"Northern California. Probably headed for Seattle. As soon as they can arrange the scheduling either Sean or Shane will go there." She made a face. "I'd go myself right now, but I don't have the weight Shane can bring to bear, or the puzzle-brain Sean has. And I need to stay close. My friend Jessie got hurt pretty badly last month, and she needs help handy."

"Jessie McBride? What happened?"

She nodded, pleased he'd remembered. But then, it seemed he remembered so much. And she again had to tamp down reading into that. "Her leg was broken, badly, in a car accident. Their ranch is right next to ours, so I'm close." She smiled. "We delivered a perfect little foal the other night."

"You always were hands-on," he said. She felt her cheeks heat as something in the way he said it reminded her of the times she'd had her hands on him. All over him. Wondered if it was a payback for her reminding him he could have had her anytime he wanted her back then.

He was silent for a moment. Then he said, "Want me to go look for him?"

Sage stared at him. "What?"

"Kane. I mean, I'm no cop or PI, but…I could at least look, until one of your brothers could get there." He grimaced. "Not like I have anything else to do at the moment. And I need something to do."

"No job prospects?"

"Haven't really looked yet. I needed some downtime. And then this happened," he said, jabbing the air with his thumb back toward where his brother would be buried.

Sage had a sudden vision of him, standing there beside the open grave, with those people—that was how she'd always thought of his family—surrounding him. It would probably feel like being on a battlefield, outnumbered by the enemy, crippled by rules of engagement that said he couldn't fight back. And it made her stomach roil.

"So, yes or no?"

She had to pull her mind back to his completely unexpected offer. She didn't know what to think about it. The part of her that missed Kane, and worried about him every day, was saying yes, but the part of her that remembered the boy Scott had been, the life of neglect and abandonment he'd had, was saying what he needed to do here was more important. Maybe even more important to her.

"I appreciate the offer," she said slowly, "but I think that before you take off across half the country, you need to make your peace with Last Stand."

After she'd dropped him off at his car she headed for the McBride place to pick Jessie up and take her to her first outpatient physical therapy appointment. She was thinking every foot of the way about what she'd said to him about making his peace with this town she so loved and he despised. She wished she could do something, anything, that would change his mind about leaving, but she'd already spoken her piece, more than once. It obviously would take more than that. More than just words…

Something flitted into her mind. By the time she reached the McBrides' she had a glimmering of an idea. Before she went to the door of the ranch house, she pulled out her phone and wrote a group text, calling a Highwater meeting tonight. She hesitated before sending it, but decided that at least she'd be sure she'd done everything she could do, and hit the send icon.

Jessie came out on the porch on her own, wrestling with crutches, and Sage realized with a wry smile she'd gone from being with the most stubborn person she knew—outside of her brothers—to the second most stubborn. She was glad of the distraction, because it helped her shove Scott out of her mind.

Or so she thought. But when she stopped at the post office to pick up a new supplement she wanted to try for Poke, and kill some time before going back to pick Jessie up, she found herself staring at the glass display case in the lobby. At the flyer about the at-risk youth riding program over in Whiskey River. Run by Kelsey Kilcoyne, wife of children's author Declan Kilcoyne, aka Declan Bolt, the program had grown exponentially since the world-famous writer had begun to take part in it. Sage admired him opening up and sharing with the kids a childhood that often made their own look mild by comparison.

The success of the program spoke for itself, and it was gaining a reputation throughout the state. And she couldn't help wondering if such a program might have helped Scott. Not that his parents would have let him go; to acknowledge there was a problem would have meant to acknowledge their part in it, and that would never have happened.

She snapped out of the reverie she seemed to be slipping into all too often since he'd come home. *Come back. Not home. Last Stand would never be his home again.*

She finished her errands with a forced briskness, loaded the groceries she'd picked up—including the salt Sean had forgotten to get last week when it had been his turn—and glanced at her phone for the time. Perfect; Jessie should be done, so she'd only have to wait the five minutes it would take Sage to get there.

On the thought, the cell in her hand startled her by letting out Jessie's ringtone. The theme song from the cartoon show they'd loved to watch together as children always made her smile, and she swiped to answer.

"Hey, I have another ride home so you don't need to

come get me."

"I don't mind."

"I know, and I appreciate it. But you've got enough to do, dealing with Scott coming home." *Last Stand would never be his home again.* It was becoming a mantra. "Besides I met someone at the physical therapist's and we're going to have pie. He said he'd bring me home after."

"Aha. Anyone I know?"

"Asher Chapman. He's from Whiskey River."

"Chapman? Is he related to Levi Chapman?"

"I have no idea. Why?"

"You know. Levi Chapman, the billionaire from Whiskey River. He's also part owner of the Devil's Rock airport."

"Oh. I didn't think about him. It's possible."

Sage couldn't resist. "Is he cute?"

There was a telling moment of silence before Jessie sighed and said, "No, he's ridiculously hot."

"Oooh, even better. Why was he there?"

"He lost one of his legs in Iraq. Below the knee. He was there to fit a new prosthetic. But I didn't know that at first. He tried to open the door for me and I was really rude."

Sage laughed. "Poor guy. I bet you gave him the 'I can do it myself!' reaction."

"You know me too well. I did."

"What did he do?"

"He let me. Then he called me grumpy."

Sage chuckled. "I like him already."

"So do I. Here he comes. I gotta go. I'll talk to you later."

"Okay, I'll expect details."

"I might even give them to you."

Sage laughed then. When they ended the call, she was smiling. Jessie had been a rock for her in those days by the creek with Scott. She'd covered for her more than once, empathized when Sage battled with her frustration at not being able to do enough to help him. She deserved the best, and this was the first spark of interest she'd heard from her about a new guy in a long time.

While you can't get past the old guy, even though you know he's going to leave again.

Chapter Sixteen

SCOTT WAS STILL pondering Sage's words as he unlocked his car and thought about what to do now. She had dropped him off here, and he told himself she had not sounded regretful about having to leave him to take her friend Jessie to her appointment.

What the hell did she mean, make his peace with Last Stand? If she meant stop hating it, he figured not thinking about it at all was pretty much the same thing, and he accomplished that most of the time. It was only in his head now, churning things up, because he was in the damn place.

So now he had a long afternoon stretching out before him, in the last place he wanted to be. Encountering his father and brother in town had convinced him walking around Last Stand was not what he wanted to do. But going back to his motel room and holing up didn't appeal; he was long done with hiding from the people he shared genes—albeit not the right ones—with.

Shooting had taken the edge off—and shooting that treasured M1 with such history had truly been an honor—but he was still restless. What he needed was something physical to do, and he pondered hitting his room, changing clothes, and running a few miles. He'd settled on that and was mentally planning a route as he opened the driver's door. It was then that the big, white building a couple of blocks down caught his eye. And he changed his mind.

Father Nunes, clad in worn work clothes and dusted with sawdust, welcomed him with a smile, which widened when he asked if he wanted that help they'd talked about.

"I need some work to do. Something else to think about," Scott said.

"And the strength to get through tomorrow?" the priest suggested.

Scott blinked. "It always amazes me," he said wryly, "how everybody in this town seems to know everything."

"I'm hurt," the man said in a tone of umbrage that was clearly mocking. "Here I thought it was just my extraordinary powers of perception."

"At least you're not claiming divine information," Scott quipped back.

"Would that it worked that way." This time the man's exaggerated sigh made him laugh. "But work I can definitely supply. No payment besides my thanks and a rather tasteless ham sandwich for lunch, I'm afraid."

"Thanks'll do. I downed a huge plate of Valencia's huevos rancheros late this morning."

"An excellent choice," the man said. "Do any carpentry in the service?"

"I was a Marine. We did everything with nothing."

That got him a wide smile. And the man ushered him inside.

The work of building shelves and storage for this room—which was to be a meeting space for various groups attached to the church—turned out to be exactly what Scott had needed. And the satisfaction of watching the work progress had eased both the knot in his gut and the turmoil in his mind. And Father Nunes was a whistle while you work kind of guy—a very good one—and Scott found himself trying to guess if the tunes he was hearing were actual songs or if the man was simply making it up as he went. Deciding if they were songs, they were probably hymns he'd never heard, he decided to just enjoy the man's artistry.

That is until, when they'd finished the last set of shelves, the man started on a clearly discernable version of the Marine Corps hymn. Startled, Scott stopped midstroke of the hammer and looked over his shoulder at the man, who finished the tune and then grinned at him.

"I particularly like those last lines, about if the Army and Navy ever get to heaven, they'll find the streets guarded by Marines."

Scott grinned back. "Yes, sir."

Feeling comfortably tired now, Scott thought he had at least a chance of getting some sleep tonight. Maybe. But by noon tomorrow the ordeal would be over, the funeral done, and he'd be able to get back to his life. That he wasn't at all sure what that life was going to entail didn't matter at this moment.

"You will get through it," Father Nunes promised him as he helped clean up after the very productive afternoon's work.

"I will. Thank you." Scott turned to go, but paused when the man added, "Feel welcome on Sunday, should you feel the need."

It was as close as the man had come to proselytizing, so Scott merely shrugged. "I leave on Sunday. Or tomorrow, if I can manage it."

The man studied him for a moment. "And not a moment too soon, I suspect?"

"You've got that right," Scott said, and it was heartfelt.

"Do you believe in redemption, Scott?"

"Maybe," he answered warily, a little nervous about hearing the word from a priest.

"Then perhaps you should give it a chance here, in your hometown."

He laughed, sharp and short. "I'll never be redeemed in the eyes of this town."

"I didn't mean you. I meant give Last Stand a chance to redeem itself in your eyes." Scott stared at the man. And this time, unexpectedly, it was the priest who shrugged. "I don't know the whole story, but I sense you were as much a victim as your brothers, just in a different way."

"I'm no victim," Scott said sharply. And the other man smiled.

"No, you are not. Not anymore."

A little to his surprise, he did sleep that night, at least enough to function. He'd done worse on less, he thought as he got up Saturday morning and hit the shower. Although if he hadn't been where he'd been and done what he'd had to do, he might have trouble believing that.

He would, as the priest had said, get through this. Somehow. It belatedly occurred to him exactly what he was likely to hear today, some recitation of his brother's life that ignored the waste of it. He would never deny that Pete had had the worst of luck, but hearing the fiction that he'd handled it with grace and courage would be a bit hard to stomach. He hoped they would at least credit the true courage in the family, that of Robbie, who had let himself be used time and again only to see it all squandered in the most dissolute way.

His first thought, when he'd found out Pete was dead, was to wonder how Robbie was going to feel now. Would he feel liberated? Or used up?

More likely used and tossed aside, if I know the old man. And I do.

Belatedly he wondered what Robbie did, if whatever job he had—Scott had no idea what it might be—would be any solace, now that the demands he give up bits and pieces of himself would cease. Or did he even work? Perhaps the parents took care of him the way a rancher took care of his prize livestock, keeping him healthy and more importantly compliant.

You know, if you're still bitter, and if you stay that way, you're letting them win.

Sage's words rang in his head, but he fought them down. He wasn't bitter, not like she meant it, because he'd told her the truth: most of the time he never even thought about them. The problem with that was that to put them out of his mind he'd had to try doing the same to her, because she was so solidly linked to Last Stand just as his unpleasant memories were, and thinking of one brought on the other. He'd gotten pretty good at shutting it down though, when those thoughts of her threatened to spiral into the rest of what haunted him about this place.

She was the only part of it he truly regretted. The only thing from Last Stand that he missed, that he wished he hadn't had to leave behind.

He dressed quickly, calculating the time so that he could slide in at the last moment. He'd pondered going in full dress uniform, but somehow showing up wearing every ribbon and medal he'd earned seemed far too much like the old Scott, pleading for the attention of people who barely noticed he was breathing. But Pete didn't deserve a suit and tie, either. Fortunately it had gotten down to thirty-seven last night, and was still chilly enough for the black pullover sweater he'd brought. That and black jeans and boots would do. His father would find it insulting, but then he'd find Scott's very presence, even though he demanded it, insulting. A fact that Scott found oddly pleasing.

He did as Sage had suggested and parked close to the gravesite rather than the chapel. It meant a bit of a walk now, but he figured he'd count it well worth it when the time came and he couldn't stomach any more.

His father was outside the small chapel, greeting the arrivals in that imperial manner he'd passed on—or taught—to his eldest son, his treasured namesake. His mother was beside him, scanning the arrivals, no doubt counting because that's what would be important to her. He thought the black-veiled hat a bit much, but then she'd always gone for the grand gesture.

And as always, Robbie was next to them, although there was more space between them. Scott wondered if that was significant, but told himself not to read anything into it.

His father saw him, but as had happened at the flower shop, there was no recognition. His mother, however, gasped, and grabbed at her husband's arm as if she needed the support. He wasn't sure how that made him feel, that she, at least, recognized him.

And then Robbie saw him. "Scott! You came. Thanks."

His brother crossed the two yards between them quickly and shook his hand, clapping him on the shoulder as he did so. With the excellent peripheral vision that had saved him more than once, Scott rather enjoyed his father's look of shock. And when Robbie stepped aside, he looked at the man and said with all the casual amusement he could muster, "Problem, Dad?"

He chose the appellation purposely, because there had never been a man who deserved it less—and because Peter Parrish Sr. had always demanded a respectful "Father."

The man stared at him, and Scott had a moment to savor his apparent speechlessness. He could almost see him recalling their encounter in town. But in nearly the same moment his father's gaze shifted, and by his expression Scott gathered someone of import was approaching, someone his mother would no doubt consider a coup, because that's how she gauged her own value.

"Chief Highwater," his mother gushed. "How wonderful

of you to come. We thank you."

Scott barely managed not to whirl around. Sage's brother was here?

And then he heard the familiar deep voice, only now it held a touch of ice. "We're not here for you. We're here for the son who deserves the support."

"Peter would so appreciate—"

"Not Peter," another male voice said, just as coolly.

"Or Robbie," said another, "although he deserves it more than Peter."

He couldn't stop himself then, he looked. Just in time to see seven people lining up in a semicircle at his back.

The Highwaters. All of them, including a petite redhead he guessed must be Lily next to Shane, who was beyond imposing in uniform and his standard dark gray cowboy hat. Sean, the brother he hadn't seen yet since he'd been back, standing with the tall, elegant woman from the restaurant, both of them clad in black, Sean with the black hat Scott remembered he'd always worn. Joey from the library standing with Slater, the only Highwater with a beard and sans the cowboy hat.

And Sage.

He stared at her. He'd never seen her like this, dressed sleekly in a slim black skirt and blouse, with gleaming black cowboy boots on her feet, and her own black cowboy hat with her long, dark hair tucked up under it. A simple pair of black pearl earrings finished it off perfectly, and his throat tightened as he remembered one day when they'd had one of those talks, about how he'd always felt the odd one out and

Sage had said, "So are black pearls, but they're the most beautiful to me."

He suddenly didn't know what to do, how to be. He'd come here feeling the odd one out yet again, the scapegrace, the black sheep, and all of a sudden he was the one with the Highwaters, one of the founding families of Last Stand, at his back. All because this woman, this incredible, gutsy, determined woman had called out the troops.

Sage stepped up to his father, and Scott saw the determined set of her jaw. "We feel for Robbie, but that's all. We're not here to honor the one who threw away all the gifts he was given. We're here for the one who made the most of the only chance he ever got. The one you threw away, but who became a hero anyway."

Chapter Seventeen

SHE COULDN'T HAVE scripted it any better.

Sage could have—and later would—hug every one of her extended family. Her brothers had come through for her as they always had—Shane even donning his dress uniform when she'd explained Scott's mother set store by appearances and position—and Lily, Joey, and Elena had never hesitated. For a moment she even teared up with her gratitude for this family she had.

The kind of family Scott had never had, but who had allied themselves with him now. For her sake, but for his, too, because they all knew now who he really was. All the Highwaters, even those who didn't yet bear the name, had a very strong respect for those who overcame adversity, because they knew what it took.

And they were still doing it. After the service, where they had presented a united front around Scott, a few people had approached rather tentatively. And every time, one of her family had made certain they were drawn in, and that somewhere during the conversation what Scott had accomplished was brought up. She herself spent some time happily bragging about his record and his status as a genuine hero.

Until Scott, looking utterly embarrassed, called a halt the first moment the eight of them were alone again.

"I...stop. Thank you, all of you, but..." They all turned to look at him. "I appreciate you...I didn't..." He stopped, swallowed, and tried again. "This means more to me than I can say, but please, stop."

"The mark of a true hero is that he doesn't think he deserves the title," Slater observed in his philosophical way.

But they heeded his wishes, and after the burial—during which Sage watched several people looking at Scott curiously but with respect, and better yet his father staring at him in obvious shock—it was Elena who shepherded them toward the cars, saying a full lunch spread would be waiting in the family dining room at Valencia's. Sage sensed Scott's resistance and leaned over to whisper, "Mrs. Valencia is overseeing it. Do you want her on your ass?"

She got the feeling he was reeling a little, because he didn't fight her when she suggested he ride with her, and she'd bring him back for his rental car later. When they were alone, she asked him, "What did you say to Robbie there at the end? He looked stunned."

Scott shrugged. "I told him if he ever wanted to get out of the cage they had him in, he could come to me and we'd figure something out."

Emotion surged in her. Impulsively she reached out and grabbed his hand. "That was a good thing to do."

He didn't look at her. Instead he stared at her hand. Their hands. And slowly his fingers curled around hers, and an entirely different kind of emotion surged through her.

The kind born of heat and need and too long without.

The kind only he had ever stirred in her.

"He didn't ask for this," he said, his voice so rough she couldn't help wondering if he was feeling the same thing. "And he handled it with the kind of grace Pete never had. That I never would have."

"Even if it was for the wrong reasons, he felt valued by your parents. You never did."

He was still staring at their hands. "Does that excuse me? What I did, how I acted?"

"The Highwaters have never been big on excuses. But it certainly explains why you were the way you were."

He was silent for a moment. He didn't let go of her hand. "I used to wonder sometimes, how I'd react. If I'd be any better than Pete, facing possibly imminent death so young. I mean, the first time he probably didn't even realize what it meant, he was only four, but he was nine when he had the relapse. He understood then."

This was something the Scott she'd known, the boy who had been hurting so badly, would never have said. He probably wouldn't have had the capacity to think about it, so much of his energy had been taken up just surviving.

"And instead of making up for how he'd been, he became a worse jerk than ever," she said. "Besides, I think you've already proven repeatedly how you'd react to facing death at a young age. Heroically."

His fingers tightened around hers. She wished she wasn't driving, because she wanted to see his face, look into those green eyes. "You didn't really have to give everybody there the whole list," he said, his voice rough again.

"Sure I did," she said cheerfully. "I spent all night memorizing it, so I was for darn sure going to use it."

This time the silence was longer, and they were back in town when he said, "You'd better let go of my hand."

"You're the one holding on," she pointed out. "Why don't you let go?"

"I can't," he whispered, so low she barely heard it.

It was a good thing the next driveway was for Valencia's, because she suddenly couldn't focus on anything but the feel of his hand and the sound of that helpless whisper.

"Is this what it's always like?" Scott asked. "Everybody laughing and talking?"

Sean Highwater grinned at him. "Pretty much. It's gotten a bit noisier and more confusing as we've grown, but this is pretty typical."

Scott watched Elena de la Cova getting people settled at the big table Sage had told him about. "She's incredibly beautiful."

"Yes, she is." Sean gave him a rather sheepish look. "I used to think of her as the Queen of Last Stand."

"She's got the air," Scott agreed, which earned him another grin. And as he thought it, the woman approached him.

"If you do not mind," she said, "my son would like to sit beside you."

He blinked. "I...okay." He'd noticed the kid, who looked about ten or eleven, in a deep conversation with Sean after they'd first arrived, but he hadn't realized he was Elena's son.

"He is normally shy around new people, but his late father was in the Army," Elena explained quietly, "so he is curious about another military man."

Scott remembered what Sage had said, felt the far too familiar sinking sensation in his gut. "Sage told me. He was KIA?"

She nodded. He saw the also too-familiar grief shadow her eyes for a moment, and glanced at Sean. Realized he had taken Elena's hand and was holding it, much as Sage had taken his. Clearly these two had reached an accord on this particular tragedy.

He closed his eyes for a moment, bowed his head, although he said nothing. But when he opened his eyes again, he saw in both Elena's and Sean's faces that they understood the silent tribute.

It was odd, he thought. He never, ever would have expected to find a group like this here. He'd always been a bit in awe of the Highwaters, even Sage, because of how they pulled together in the face of their own tragedies. They had become an even more solid unit, all of them, with no one left out or abandoned, even the brother who was missing. Even though some suspected Kane was responsible, that he'd purposely pushed his father into the path of that truck, Sage had never stopped defending her brother, just as she had never stopped defending him.

And they had never stopped looking for him. While his own parents had been glad to have him gone.

Even as he thought about parents, Elena's mother was there. He recognized her immediately, both by memory and resemblance to her daughter. He looked rather warily at the woman who had been the most intimidating teacher he or almost anyone at Creekbend High School had ever had. But she was smiling at him.

"I knew you had it inside you, to become what you've become," she said.

He swallowed. "I...thank you. I heard you told Chief Highwater that back then."

"I did. And my dear cousin, the judge. I knew you had a good mind, it was simply your situation that had you out of control."

He gave her a wry smile. "That's putting a nicer face on it than I deserve."

The woman who was the living prototype for her daughter—it must be strange for Sean to see what Elena would probably look like in thirty years—drew back slightly. "I see you haven't quite broken that habit. A certain amount of self-deprecation is charming, young Parrish, but not to the extent of denying what is obvious to all of us."

It was spoken in the steely voice he remembered, and he knew better than to contest it. "Yes, ma'am," he said meekly.

To his surprise the older woman laughed delightedly. "Oh, yes, you'll do."

Do for what, Scott wasn't sure. But for the moment he simply sat, enjoyed the delicious meal, marveled at the openness and chatter around the table, so different from the stiff, stilted, and sternly enforced silence he'd grown up with. And when he caught young Marcos watching him surreptitiously, but still not having said a word to him, he pretended to have no idea that you were supposed to unwrap a tamale before eating it and the boy laughingly showed him how to peel open the corn husks.

That broke the dam and the boy was a constant stream of questions from then on. When Scott realized that the rest of the table had fallen almost silent, he looked up to find them all looking at him with approval and wide smiles. He felt a strange burst of something it took him a moment to identify, so unexpected was it here. But it was the same sense he'd had about the eighth week of the Scout Sniper Basic course, a sense of belonging.

There and then, it had made him proud. Here and now he dodged it, because deep down he knew he didn't belong here. These people were warm and welcoming, but this was still Last Stand and he'd put this place behind him years ago. He shoved the emotion aside; he was feeling a longing for how it could have been but never was, which seemed the biggest waste of time there could be. Although at this rate it would be late before he was able to hit the road for Austin and his escape.

And belatedly it hit him it was over. The funeral was done. It had gone—thanks to Sage and these people who would clearly do anything for each other—better than he could ever have hoped, and now he was free. Free to go on with his life. Or at least free to figure out what it was going to be. Free to choose his path. Free to do what he'd planned to do from the moment he'd decided to come back and pay the debts he felt he owed.

To put Last Stand where it belonged, in his rearview mirror, for the very last time.

Chapter Eighteen

SCOTT STEPPED OUT of the convenience store where he'd stopped to pick up a sandwich and some chips for the drive back to the airport. He'd ended up going back to the original plan to leave today instead of right after the funeral. Not, he told himself firmly, because he wanted to stay, but because he'd been too tired to safely drive.

And because he had the biggest task yet still before him…heading out to the ranch to say a final goodbye to Sage. And he dreaded that more than he'd ever dreaded anything, even in a war zone.

His gut knotted up as it had been doing all morning.

Compartmentalize. Don't think about what's ahead, just think about what has to be done now.

The mantra had gotten him through ten years in uniform, but it seemed to be falling sadly short now. Yet it had to be done. He'd already been out to their place on the creek, in a no doubt futile effort to make up for the way he'd left last time. And as insurance, because he had little doubt he would never manage to put into words what he was feeling when he was face-to-face with her. But he would tell her to go there, and—

He let go of the door and nearly walked into Lily Jones.

"Just the man I was looking for," she said cheerfully. He liked that she didn't assume he was in a funk because they'd just buried his brother yesterday.

"Uh...good morning?"

She smiled. "It is lovely." She glanced at what he held. "Stocking up?"

"For the drive to Austin."

There was a pause so brief he couldn't be sure it meant anything before she said, "Then I caught you just in time."

"For what?" he asked, his eyebrows lowering warily.

"I wanted to talk to you about a series of articles I'm doing." She grinned widely, and Scott saw why she had the chief so entranced. It wasn't just that she was beautiful, but intelligence and humor gleamed in her eyes. "I'll even buy breakfast. How about a big slice of the best bee sting cake in Texas?"

He remembered the almond, honey, and custard treat from Kolaches, the German bakery, and couldn't deny his stomach woke up at the suggestion. He rarely indulged in such things, but on this quiet Sunday morning it sounded...irresistible. But he was still wary. "Why would you want to talk to me?"

"Why do you think?"

"I have no idea."

She smiled. "And that's why."

He blinked. Then, rather wryly, he said, "I'll bet you keep even the chief on his toes."

"I try," she said airily. "Deal?"

He'd been thinking he'd start toward Austin now, and kill his extra time at the airport, but what the heck. It wasn't like she was actually a Highwater—yet—and he'd only just met her so she wouldn't be constantly reminding him of Sage. He was curious what she could be working on that she'd want to talk to him about. And there was that German treat, something he'd only had once but had been good enough that he remembered it.

So they ended up walking toward the bakery, down Main Street from the city quad, fronted by the courthouse where he'd gone to see Judge Morales, the library where Joey worked, and where the statue of town hero Asa Fuhrmann stood.

"So what's this about?" he asked, after he'd tested the sweet layers that were as good as he remembered, although just as tricky to eat because the caramelized almonds on top were solid enough that it mashed the layers beneath when you tried to stick a fork in it.

"I'm writing a series of articles for *The Defender*, which has been picked up by a news service and is going nationwide."

"Congratulations," he said tentatively, still not seeing a connection.

"They're profiles, actually, and they've been quite popular."

"Profiles?"

She nodded. "Called 'Hometown Heroes.'" She nodded out the window toward the statue. "I started with him, obviously."

He thought he got it then, what she wanted to talk to him about. He remembered glancing at the figure of the man who had sacrificed his life to make Last Stand possible. The statue Scott had seen while still overseas, when Cindy had been showing him the series of videos and images of Shane Highwater.

"I heard about the crash last year on Mrs. Herdmann's birthday. And what the chief did, pulling that guy out of the fire."

"Yes. Just months after he landed in the hospital doing the same thing."

"Wow. I didn't know that."

"Long story that I'll tell you later if you want."

"So you want to ask about what he did for me? For his profile?"

She smiled at him, knowingly but with a touch of amusement. "Your modesty is quite becoming."

He drew back slightly. "What?"

"Oh, I'm going to write about Shane, as soon as I figure out how to write the disclaimer that it might be biased because I am mad, crazy in love with him."

"I noticed," Scott said, but he smiled when he said it.

"Which, considering I was out to destroy him not so long ago, is saying something."

Scott blinked. "You...what?"

"That other crash he tried to pull someone out of? The driver was my then fiancé."

Scott gaped at her. "Holy..."

"Indeed. Also part of that long, and if I say so myself,

fascinating story I'd be happy to tell you someday."

Someday. But there wouldn't be a someday for him, not in Last Stand. By this evening he'd be on a plane back to California, to the apartment off base near Pendleton, where he would... He had no idea what he would do. But he'd find something. He couldn't bunk with his buddies forever.

"But now," Lily said, keeping her eyes on him steadily, "I'm focusing on you." He went still, suddenly not liking where he thought this might be heading. "Scott Parrish, one of the most impressive true heroes Last Stand has turned out."

"Me?" He almost yelped it.

"You."

"Come on, you've got famous baseball players, rodeo riders, race car drivers—"

Lily cut him off with a shake of her head. "Celebrities."

"Then you've got doctors who save lives, like the McBrides—"

"I've done Doc McBride, Turner and Graham and Spencer—he's a paramedic—are on the list. And Jessie, for that matter, for her work rescuing mustangs. But I'm willing to bet when it comes to saving lives, you have almost everyone beat. Because you saved nearly a thousand at one time."

He stared at her. That incident wasn't in the file he'd shown the chief, or Judge Morales. He'd made sure of it. "How did you—"

"—know that you stopped an attack on a village with over nine hundred innocent refugees? I used to be a reporter, Scott. There are ways."

"Whoever told you—"

"Agrees with me. They don't hand out those Bronze Stars for nothing, Scott. Or Purple Hearts."

"I was just a guy doing his job. Like thousands of others."

"But better than most."

He shook his head.

She smiled again, as if she'd expected it. "Boy, Shane has you pegged. Will you settle for better than many?"

He was starting to feel a little beleaguered. "There are a lot of people from here who deserve this more than I do."

"It's true, Last Stand has turned out more than its share of notable heroes, given our size, but it's also true you're among the best of those. You can deny it all you want, but the facts are what they are." She grinned again now. "Pesky thing, facts."

He tried a diversion. "Some journalists don't think so. Some just ignore them if they get in the way."

"Or make them up," she agreed easily. "Or in my case, think we have the whole story when we don't." He had the feeling that had something to do with what she'd said about being out to destroy the chief. But she didn't give him time to ponder that. "Tell me why you're so reluctant to do this. Is it because you don't like blowing your own horn?"

And suddenly he was back at Sage again, remembering her telling the range master about his record, and his remark about blowing his own horn. "Damn," he muttered.

"Wouldn't you like to show everyone how wrong they were? Especially your parents?"

He couldn't deny it was tempting. But he'd spent ten years convincing himself they didn't matter.

They don't matter, Scott. It's who you are, inside, in spite of them that matters.

And again he was back to Sage, and he could hear the urging, almost pleading in her voice at a time when he'd been closer to the edge than ever before. She'd saved him yet again then.

"Shane thinks you don't talk about your military career because you don't think Last Stand will believe you turned out so well."

Feeling more than a little cornered now, he muttered, "Where is the local sex symbol anyway?"

He'd thought she might take offense, but instead she burst out laughing. "Oh, he's way beyond local these days. And he hates every second of it."

He was…not really surprised, but interested. "A lot of guys would love it."

"Sure. But not Shane. Probably for some of the same reasons you're reluctant to do this. He's a confident, exceptionally competent and courageous man, but he doesn't see himself as anything special. And neither, apparently, do you."

"I'm not."

"Good thing the rest of us know better, then. So tell me about—"

She broke off as the door to the bakery swung open. Scott knew without looking who it was, simply by the way her face lit up. He felt that ache deep down that he'd felt so often since he'd made the mistake of coming back to this damn town that wouldn't seem to let go. And then it hit him to wonder if they were all here, in town. If he'd have to say goodbye to Sage here, where he least wanted to.

Better that than missing her because you went to the ranch and she was here.

He braced himself, expecting not just Shane but all of them. But the chief didn't come inside. Scott turned to look. The man was grinning. "You might want to see this, Parrish. My sister just ran into your folks."

He felt a chill and was on his feet and heading for the door before he thought. "If he says anything malicious to her—"

"Whoa, there." The man blocked him with an arm he was tempted for an instant to break. But only an instant, not just because he was the chief and in the kind of shape that said he could probably match him blow for blow, but because he was Sage's brother. And belatedly he realized that also meant he wouldn't be amused if she was in any real trouble. "My sister doesn't need any help. She can hold her own against a lot worse than those two miserable excuses for parents. Let her deal." He grinned again. "But it's worth watching."

Scott tried to process that this man, of all people, was rather gleeful about his sister apparently confronting his parents. He looked down the street. Spotted them. Saw the confused looks on both their faces.

Saw the fiery anger in Sage's.

And he couldn't have moved if he'd wanted to.

Chapter Nineteen

THEY WERE ONE door down, in front of Yippee Ki Yay, the western store, but Scott could hear them clearly. Especially his father's derisive voice.

"—always a troublemaker, causing problems."

"He's just bad," his mother chimed in, as she always did.

"You really don't get it, do you? Why he acted as he did?" Sage said, the incredulity in her tone obvious even from here. Scott glanced again at her brother, who shook his head. With an effort, he stayed put as his father spoke again, in that same ugly voice.

"He was envious of his brother, because Peter was so much better than him. And then when Peter got sick, he was jealous of all the attention he got."

"Jealous? Of course he was jealous, you stupid fools! Do you think he didn't know you bred him for replacement parts, like some dystopian science fiction novel? That you never loved him, not the way a son should be loved? I care a hundred times more for my horses than you ever cared about him!"

"Now see here—"

"I see perfectly. And so will everybody else in Last Stand

when they learn the truth of what he's done, the hero he's become, even after the horrible way you, both of you"—Sage glared at his mother—"treated him. Things are going to change, *Mister* Parrish."

His father gave her a scoffing glare. "He's a pariah. He will always be a pariah."

"Not when the truth comes out. About him and about you, both of you. Do you think he doesn't know you tried to get rid of him? That when you found out he wasn't a match to your precious Peter you tried to give him away?"

Scott's breath caught for a moment; he'd never told them he knew, that he'd found those papers. And they both looked utterly stunned that she knew. Or maybe that she had dared to publicly confront them with it.

"We didn't do it!" his father said sharply.

"But you intended to. Why did you change your mind after you found out you had a sacrificial lamb?" Sage asked. "Decide it would look bad, if you kept Robbie but dumped Scott?"

Scott went tense. His father looked furious, but his mother was…damn, she was blushing. He thought, trying to remember. She was right. Shit, she was right. Those papers had been dated shortly after he knew they'd learned Robbie was a donor match. He'd never put that together before. Leave it to Sage…who was barreling on.

"All you ever had to do was include him in the fight and he would have been there for all of you—he's proven that a hundred times over with what he's accomplished since you drove him away."

"Those are just tales he's telling," his mother said, with a wave of her hand, clearly recovered now. "To make himself seem better."

Lily's voice came from behind him, soft and quiet. "And now you know why this piece is getting written. I'd like it to be with your input, but it's getting written either way."

Scott heard her, but he couldn't take his eyes off of Sage as she stood there, facing down the two people who had shaped him. "And unlike you, I'll respect your grief and leave it at that. But I can't help wishing it was the old days when my brother could tell you to get out of town."

"She just never quits…"

Scott was barely aware of saying it out loud until her brother answered quietly, "Sage has always been the best of us at walking in another's shoes. Like yours. Like Kane's. She jokes she only understands horses, but the truth is she understands people better than most of us."

As he said it Sage turned her back abruptly on his parents and started walking toward them, her jaw set so tightly he knew it was to hold back another flood of angry words. She looked just as she had whenever he'd told her of the latest tirade his father had unleashed on him back then.

"I think she's earned her own piece of cake, don't you?" Lily said, lightening the mood.

"The biggest one they've got," Scott said lowly, watching her in the moments before she looked up and saw him. "The whole damn thing, if she wants it."

"And that interview?"

"You've got it," he said. If Sage could do what she'd just

done, the least he could do was open up to a reporter who at least thought him worth something.

And then she spotted him. Her steps faltered, but only for an instant. He had the oddest feeling she wanted to run to him, but then she steadied herself and held her same pace. But she kept coming.

And when she got to them, heedless of being out here on Main Street on a crowded tourist Sunday, she hugged him. And the moment he felt her arms go around him, the moment his body slammed awake at the feel and heat of her, he lost it.

And he kissed her.

It was a thank you kind of kiss, he told himself in the instant before their lips touched. She'd stood down the pair that had made his life hell, in full view of everyone, even though she had to know it would be the talk of Last Stand within an hour.

But the moment he felt her lips beneath his any idea this was a mere thank-you vanished, seared to ash by the heat that exploded to life. Just as did any awareness of where they were, and who was standing just behind him. The brother who had once stood between them.

And then she was kissing him back, tasting, giving, his pulse was hammering in his ears and parts of him he hadn't heard from in a while were rising to the occasion so fast it sucked the breath right out of him. And he dimly realized he was within an inch of pushing her up against the doorjamb so he could feel her body pressed to his.

Vaguely he heard a catcall from down the street, and

then a loud whistle from the other direction.

And with one of the greater efforts of his life he broke the kiss. But he didn't, couldn't let go of her. Not when she was looking at him as if she'd felt everything he had in these hot, searing moments.

Then someone yelled, "Still getting in trouble, huh, Parrish?"

It finally penetrated that they—or rather he—had drawn a lot of attention. Once again the talk of Last Stand…

"I think we'll pretend we didn't see that," her brother said, and he and Lily vanished back into the bakery.

For a long moment Sage stood looking up at him. He couldn't find a single word in all the words he knew, English and otherwise, that he could manage to speak.

He'd kissed her before. More than once, in those days down by the creek.

He'd convinced himself it hadn't really been like he remembered. That it hadn't been an instant inferno, that his imagination was coloring his memory, that the fact that he missed her so brutally was painting it as brighter, hotter, and better than it had been.

He knew better now.

He'd wondered if Last Stand would even remember him at all.

He knew better now.

He'd somehow thought that leaving would be easier this time.

He knew better now.

Chapter Twenty

SAGE TRIED TO hammer it into her brain that he was leaving. He'd made it clear from the beginning, and the fact that his flight was today, the very next day after the funeral, told her he'd meant it.

But knowing it and accepting it were two different things.

And thinking that kiss—that hot, searing, consuming kiss—made any difference would be beyond foolish. He'd made that clear by the way his jaw had tightened when that idiot had yelled at them.

Sage sat there picking at the bee sting cake she normally would have devoured eagerly. When she realized she didn't want to eat it because she didn't want anything to erase the taste of him, she nearly laughed at herself.

Because he was still going to leave.

Surreptitiously she watched him, answering Lily's questions. She wasn't close enough to hear them—it was a private interview. She wasn't even sure why he was doing it, except maybe this was his one effort at proving his parents wrong, before he left Last Stand for good.

She didn't blame him. Even before that jerk had yelled at

him she'd heard the whispers, seen the sideways looks he'd gotten from all the usual suspects, the people prone to gossip and thinking the worst of other people. Funny how those two aspects always seemed to go together.

Maybe he was right, maybe they would never forget the boy he'd been, despite the man he'd become. And if he was, she understood why he couldn't stay. Wouldn't want to stay. Even for her.

And for the first time in her life, she thought about actually leaving Last Stand. The very thought would have been beyond absurd just a week ago, but now she considered it. At least enough to think about what life might be like, away from here. Away from her brothers, her friends, away from the ranch, away from the horses. And the town she loved, warts and all. Last Stand wasn't perfect, but it was the best place she'd ever been. And the idea of leaving it hurt deep inside. No, she didn't like any of those thoughts.

The only thing she liked less was the thought of losing Scott again.

What makes you think he'd even ask you to come with him anyway? You're Last Stand to him, and he's made it clear he wants no part of it.

As for the sparks that leapt to life between them, that clearly wasn't enough to change his mind.

She doubted anything was.

So now she thought about spending the rest of her life wondering what might have been. He'd pulled back to protect her at sixteen—that she at least understood, especially with her big brothers hovering ominously. She'd even been thankful, once she'd regained some equilibrium.

But now...she was no kid now. She was a woman, in charge of her own life, her own destiny. No one else made decisions for her anymore. No one told her she couldn't have what she wanted if she was willing to work hard enough to get it.

And she wanted Scott.

Any woman breathing would look at him now and understand.

Any woman who'd had him kiss her, as he just had, would figure the world well lost to keep this man.

But before she could decide what to do about it, she saw Lily close her small notebook, and in the way of a man who'd made a decision, Scott pushed back his chair and stood up. He came back to the table where she and her brother were sitting. And when he spoke, it was very formally.

"I have a plane to catch. But I want to thank you all again for making yesterday much less horrible than I assumed it would be."

He said it like a man making a speech. As perhaps he was.

Or covering all his bases, so he never, ever has to come back...

"And," he said, in the same tone, "for giving me a welcome I never expected here."

"Here," Shane said, looking up at him but not rising, "is a good place, Scott. It's not responsible for the mess your family made of your life. Don't blame Last Stand because they're a pair of…" Shane seemed to catch himself, glanced at her and then Lily, and amended whatever he'd been going to say—Sage suspected it had to do with a certain body part—to "malicious idiots."

"More like pitiful fools," Lily said, "not to see what they had in you."

Scott's jaw tightened visibly in that way Sage remembered, when he was so full of roiling emotion he didn't trust himself to speak. It had often taken her two or three tries to find the right prod, the words that would make him open up and let it out.

"If I'd known then, that you…that not everybody thought…maybe…"

"Then that is our fault," Shane said. "We should have stepped up sooner."

Scott shifted his gaze to her brother. "When you did, it changed my life. Saved my life. I owe you." He looked back at Sage and added, his voice suddenly rough again, "Both of you."

She saw the finality in his gaze. He'd done what he'd come to do, it was over, and now he could escape. Again.

"You can change that flight. Why don't you stay awhile?" Lily asked.

Sage's breath stopped. So many times she'd caught herself on the verge of asking—hell, begging—him to stay, but had stopped because of what lay between them. But it was different, wasn't it, if Lily asked? She'd only just met him, after all. There was no painful history there—maybe she just wanted the chance to talk to him longer about her profile.

But then the woman who had already given so much to the brother who asked for so little glanced at her, and Sage realized she was not asking for herself, Lily was asking for her. And in that moment Sage knew for certain what a treasure her brother had found in this woman who would soon be her sister.

"I...can't," Scott said, his voice low.

Shane leaned back in his chair. "You have someplace to be? Job to start or something?"

Sage could have kissed her big brother, not only for what he was doing but for the casual, relaxed way he was doing it. As if he knew anything more pointed or pushy would send Scott running. Of course, he hadn't become chief before spending a lot of time interviewing people who were often on the verge of doing just that.

She herself kept her mouth shut. It was true she had the most invested here, but it was also true Scott would likely respond differently—maybe even do that running—if she was the one pushing at him. Why she knew that, she wasn't sure. Maybe because she knew he felt he owed her, and sensed he was afraid she'd use that on him.

"No," Scott answered finally, looking faintly uncomfortable. "But I need to figure out what I want to do and start looking."

"Start here," Lily suggested.

A short, compressed snort of laughter burst from him. "Here? Like anyone in Last Stand would hire me."

"I would," Shane said quietly. "If you wanted to put a uniform back on."

Sage savored the sweetness of Scott staring at her brother in shock. "You...would hire me?"

"In an instant."

"But you couldn't hire somebody who got in so much trouble here—"

"Who better to recognize trouble before it starts? And I have full hiring discretion," Shane said. His mouth quirked slightly. "I'll admit, I took some heat when I hired Sean, him being my brother, but the solve rate he's racked up took care of that pretty quickly. The powers that be tend to like that they've got a guy who tops the whole state in clearance percentage."

"But that's...Sean."

Shane nodded. "And he wanted the job. It's not for everyone, and if you're tired of being the sheepdog, that's understandable. But that's just one option."

"You say that like there's a line at the door," Scott said sourly.

"I know a couple of others," Shane said. "Ranger Buckley has been talking about taking somebody on at the inn." Scott blinked at that. And Sage knew she hadn't mistaken the very slight, very brief smile that lifted one corner of his mouth.

"You think he'd take on a former trespasser?"

"I know that he sees the man that kid became, because we talked about it," Shane said.

Scott looked a little stunned again, and Sage realized just how deeply he'd been convinced that everyone in Last Stand had been glad to see the back of him and would be in no hurry to welcome him back.

"Or Mike Fleming," she burst out, unable to hold back any longer.

Scott's head turned as he looked at her. Shane said, "Oh, now there's a thought."

"The range master?" Scott said. And as Sage held her breath, he sank back down into his chair.

"He's been looking for someone to help manage the place for a while. Somebody who might take it over someday when he wants to retire," she said, working to keep her tone casual. "But he worries about finding somebody he can trust to feel the same way he does about it. He wouldn't worry about that with you."

"And if none of those suit you," Lily said cheerfully, "just put the word out, say, the day after my profile comes out."

Shane laughed and gave his fiancée a loving look. "Do that. You'll be interviewing prospective employers instead of the other way around."

"They truly will be lined up at your door," Sage agreed.

He grimaced then. "Even if that were true, I…sort of don't have a door anymore. I checked out of the motel in Whiskey River and they were already renting my room when I left."

"You shouldn't have been staying there anyway," Lily said. "You should be here in town."

"Or out at the ranch. Plenty of room there," Shane said, inviting him to stay in his home as easily as if there was no history here, or more impossibly, as if what history there was was good. At least, good by chief of police standards.

Scott looked as if he'd been hit by a sucker punch. "I

can't."

"What if I said this is what you owe me, and Sage?" Shane said quietly. "You give Last Stand another chance, and we're even." Scott didn't answer. Sage could almost feel his tension. "At least think about it."

Both Lily and Shane stood up. Lily smiled, but then, his expression turning solemn, the police chief of Last Stand said, "Sergeant," and tapped his right hand to his brow in a salute in the moment before he and Lily walked away.

It was a gesture that apparently left Scott speechless. Sage watched him across the small table, and for the first time saw a hint of uncertainty, as if his determination had been at least been dented.

She had to rein in the hope that soared inside her. Because she knew that he hadn't built the life he had by being easily dissuaded.

Chapter Twenty-One

GIVE LAST STAND another chance.
Give Last Stand a chance to redeem itself, in your eyes.
You need to make your peace with Last Stand.

Scott stared down at the last bit of coffee in his cup. What the hell was it about this place that had people championing it all the time?

He felt wound too tight, as if he had to move or the mainspring would break and he'd go flying off in a million different directions.

And he still had to say goodbye.

"Shall we get out of here, go for a walk? Down to the park?"

Sage's quiet suggestion made his gaze snap back to her face in surprise. But why he was surprised he didn't know; she'd always been able to sense when he reached this point. Just because he'd been gone for ten years didn't mean she'd lost the knack. Obviously.

"Fine," he muttered.

They walked in silence until they made the turn on Hickory and headed toward the park. Sage slowed. "Maybe this wasn't a great idea," she said, eying how many people had had the same idea this Sunday morning. "Maybe we should go sit and relax in the city courtyard. It's a lot less crowded."

"Your roots are showing," he said dryly. "Just relax, within a hundred feet of the police department?"

"So are yours, if that bothers you," she retorted.

He drew back slightly. "Good point," he admitted, and they headed that way.

They passed a half a dozen people as they walked. Two of them took one look at him and started whispering to each other furtively. Two more did blatant double takes, and a fifth frowned at him rather fiercely. The sixth ignored him completely.

I'd like a town full of number sixes, please…

They ended up having the courtyard all to themselves and sat on one of the stone benches that served as decidedly uncomfortable seating for people who had to wait for the wheels of government to slowly grind.

"Did you ever know Lark Leclair?" she asked, looking over toward the library building. "She was in Sean's class at school."

He blinked. She'd always been good with seeming non sequiturs, which turned out to be perfectly logical once she got to her point.

"I don't think so. I remember the name, but that's all."

"She worked for Child Services for a while, after college. And she was really good at it. Even the scared, abused kids trusted her instinctively."

He had no idea where she was going with this. Was the

past tense because it was past to him, or because...the woman was dead? Had one of those abused kids not trusted her? Was she somehow going to relate this to him, or—

"While she was working there, I asked her if the kids she had helped, the ones who had gone through hell, ever turned out okay."

He went still. Because he knew, in his gut, that she'd been thinking about him. Not with anger, as he'd always expected, but with concern. She'd still cared, even then.

"She said the strong ones, the brave ones did," Sage went on. She looked back at him then, and those incredible blue eyes were warm. "Guess you proved her right times about ten, didn't you."

It wasn't a question. She stated it as fact. He tried to swallow past the tightening in his throat. "She quit?"

"It got to her. I think she was too gentle, too kind. She felt every bit of their pain. She works for a private adoption agency now."

"And she's...happier?"

"Much."

"Good. She sounds like the kind of person who deserves to be happy."

"You're not going to stay, are you," she said. This wasn't a question either. And she sounded sad.

"I can't."

"Can't?"

He leaned forward and rested his elbows on his knees. "I can't...be that close to you." *I want you too much.*

Another long silence spun out between them. Then she

asked, "Are you still afraid of my brothers?"

He laughed, surprising himself. "Anyone who doesn't take care around a Highwater deserves what they get." He gave her a sideways look. She was smiling, which eased his tension a little. "And I mean all the Highwaters. But no, I'm not afraid of your brothers anymore."

"Then what are you afraid of?"

"You."

She looked startled. "Why?"

"You want me to stay at your house?"

"Actually, if you recall, Shane invited you."

"He might not have if he knew…what we're like together."

"What are we like together, Scott? It's my recollection we never really found out, not all the way. Because you wouldn't."

The low-level arousal he'd been feeling ever since the conversation had veered this way abruptly surged into high gear. Memories of that time, of moments by the creek when it had taken every ounce of his will to pull back from what she was offering so freely, nearly swamped him. That someone had wanted him, specifically him, so much had been beyond heady. That it had been Sage had been… He had no words for how that had made him feel then.

And now, after that impulsive kiss that had singed every nerve… He wasn't sure he had any words for it now. And he couldn't even think, over the hammering of his pulse in his ears. But she was looking at him, in that same way she had back then…

"You know what we'd be like, Sage. Hell, just kissing you was more than I ever felt with anyone else going all—" He broke off. Her gaze narrowed and he looked away. Had to look away.

When she spoke her voice was wry with a touch of amusement. "I didn't assume you'd stayed celibate for ten years."

"Might as well have," he muttered.

He heard her sigh. "I know the feeling." His gaze shot back to her face. Her brows lowered. "Don't even ask."

He wouldn't. He didn't want to know who she'd been with. Especially didn't want to know who had been her first. "You don't know how many times I wished…it had been me."

"And how would I know, since you never even communicated—" This time it was she who broke off, and again she sighed deeply. "I never realized until you came back just how sore that spot still was."

"I hurt you. Badly. You don't want me staying with you."

Her chin went up. "Didn't I tell you I don't let other people make decisions for me anymore?"

Damn, she was…incredible. All that fire and ferocity, yet gentle and caring enough to save a kid who was on the verge of exploding into disaster. And the most vivid memory of all, of her half naked in his arms, her sweet, rounded breasts in his hands, her hands stroking achingly rigid flesh through his jeans, nearly swamped him and he had to look away. It took a moment of fierce focus to rein himself in. It always had, with her. And when he spoke his voice was rough with everything he was feeling.

"Aren't you worried I'd take what I was afraid to before, and then just leave you, like everybody said I would?"

"Worried? No. I've always known the man you are at the core, Scott. But the big difference now is that I'm old enough to know—and take—what I want. And pay the price if I have to."

And the way she looked at him then made it impossible to breathe at all.

"Hey, Parrish!" He nearly jumped at the shout. Looked up to see Brock Olson, an old classmate who looked the same as he had in high school. "Heard you were back in town. Come to stir up some new trouble?"

"Would you expect any less?" he retorted.

And he sat there with the reminder echoing in his head, that as far as the rest of Last Stand was concerned, nothing had really changed.

SAGE WANTED TO throw something at that Olson clown. Talk about blowing the mood. She'd pretty much declared herself Scott's for the taking, and then he had to mouth off and ruin the moment.

She'd hoped she could add to what her family had done, convince him to stay a little longer at least, but—

"—see him back here." The female voice came from a few feet away.

"I'm surprised he even showed up for the funeral."

"Poor Wilhelmina, him turning out like that. Now she's only got the one son left."

Sage was halfway to her feet, ready to call out the two old biddies who were too cowardly to say it to his face, but made sure their voices were loud enough for him to hear as they went by. Scott took her arm, pulled her back down.

"It doesn't matter," he said. His tone made her gaze snap back to his face. And she saw that he'd already shut down. She recognized the look from the times when what his parents had said or done to him had been simply too much to process and he'd gone flat. Numb inside, he'd told her once. And she could have screamed at those two women for bringing it all crashing down on him again, the realization that for some people in Last Stand he would forever be the bad boy he'd been.

"Why do you care what they think? They don't know the truth!"

"I don't care," he said. "But that doesn't mean I want to live with it every day when I don't have to." He stopped. She heard him suck in a breath. When he spoke again, his voice was so dead she knew this would likely be the last time she would ever see him. "Thank you for coming out here with me."

He said it with a tone of finality that proved she'd been right. "That's all it takes? A jerk and two nasty old ladies?"

"They're only saying what most of Last Stand is thinking. Look, I just I didn't want it to be like last time. When I didn't see you or talk to you."

"I'm not sure that makes it easier," Sage said, desperately trying to think of something, anything to change what was happening.

"I don't deserve it to be easy."

"Stop it," she said reflexively. And a little voice inside her whispered, *See what being back here just a few days does to him? It turns him back into the kid he used to be, hurting, bleeding inside. This is why he has to leave.*

Even as she thought it, he said it. "I have to get out of here, Sage." He sounded racked, tortured, and she knew he meant it. She glanced at his face, but the pain in his eyes was more than she could take. "I wish things were different. I wish..." He stopped. Ran a hand through his hair. "God, I sound like that kid I was again. Wishing. Always wishing."

"You'll never be that trapped kid again," she said softly.

"No. But I swore when I got out of here I'd never come back. I've already broken that once."

"Because you felt you had debts to pay."

"Yes." And then he was holding a hand out to her. And on his palm lay the medal she'd given him all those years ago. Her grandfather's medal. "I carried it on every mission," he said quietly. "In my mind, this was what kept me alive."

"Keep it." She said it almost desperately, because she knew what this was, his final goodbye, the last debt paid.

He shook his head. "It's not mine."

And you aren't mine, no matter how much I want you to be. "So now all your debts are repaid, and you can't wait to leave Last Stand in the dust again."

His mouth tightened, his jaw clenched. And suddenly

Sage couldn't bear it any longer. He'd been hurt enough in his life, he didn't need her piling on. Even though it would break her heart to let him go.

"I'm sorry, Scott. I know you have to go. I know why." She sighed heavily. "If they were my family I'd feel the same way, that a world between us wasn't enough."

"I'm sorry." The words sounded as if they had been wrenched out of him with rusty pliers. Not because he was reluctant to apologize, but because, she suddenly realized, leaving was hurting him as much as it was hurting her.

But staying would probably hurt him more.

Even as she thought it he stood up. She couldn't seem to find the strength to get up herself. He looked down at her. "Check our place," he said roughly. It was the last thing she heard from him.

She didn't watch him go.

She couldn't watch him walk out of her life.

Again.

All the possibilities they'd given him, and he'd turned away.

All the love she'd offered him, and he'd turned away.

If that smartass hadn't yelled at him, if those two busybodies hadn't happened by just then, at that moment when the scales could still be tipped…would his decision have been different? He'd seemed receptive, at least. Could it all—her future and his—have truly depended on a couple of stupid, malicious moments in time? She wanted to hunt them down and scream at them. But she'd already run through her quota of confrontation for today with his parents, hadn't she?

As if there could be any limitations on her defense of the man she loved, even in the face of the amount of ridicule and derision aimed at him.

Come to stir up some new trouble?

He's just bad.

He was envious of his brother, because he was so much better.

Poor Wilhelmina, him turning out like that. Now she's only got the one son left.

Their cruel words rang in her head. Who was she to tell him he should come back here and live with that?

She was barely aware when someone approached, and she only glanced as the person sat down on the bench beside her.

Elena.

"You get elected to come find me?" she asked, trying not to sound bitter and not completely succeeding.

"I volunteered," the woman said, her dark eyes glowing with a sympathy Sage was in no mood for. "Everyone agreed I might be best suited for it."

She blinked at that. "Why?"

Elena didn't answer her question, but what she did ask made Sage forget she had asked. "Does he know you love him?"

"Of course."

Elena gave her a wry smile. "Let me rephrase, as someone who had to go to some effort to convince Sean of my feelings. Have you *told* him? Actually said the words?"

"I…"

She had not. But he had to know, didn't he? Would she have tried so hard to convince him to stay if she didn't? Surely he realized that?

"I would think," Elena said in that decorous way of hers, "that a man such as Scott, who suffered what he did at the hands of those who should have loved him, might need to hear it spoken. Perhaps repeatedly."

It made sense, but... "I'm not sure he'd believe it."

"Perhaps you're right. He's never been able to count on the love most of us have from birth, that of our parents. I would guess he knows little about true, lasting love. He might not believe it until it is shown to him, proven."

"You're right," she breathed, feeling a chill at the thought that it had been her own lack that had driven him away as much as the taunts of some in Last Stand.

"This, at least, can be fixed, then," Elena said briskly, standing up. "And," she added, watching Sage with a serene smile as she also stood, "I have complete faith that you can do so."

There had been a time when she would have hesitated to embrace the elegant, refined Elena, but she hugged her now with certainty. "My brother is so lucky. And so are we, that he brought you home to us."

Elena was smiling widely when Sage stepped back. "If you need any help," she began.

"I'll send up a flare."

She was halfway to the ranch before Scott's last words to her replayed in her head.

Check our place.

In an instant she made a U-turn and headed back toward Hickory Creek. And a somewhat reckless few minutes later she was sitting on the ledge above the water, staring at the letter she had pulled out of the hiding place, noticing he'd made sure this time, sealing it in a plastic bag.

It took more nerve than she would have imagined it could to unfold the page. And even more to begin to read.

Dearest Sage,

I love you.

That may be the only part of this that matters. I can't re-create what I wrote ten years ago, just as I can't go back and do it differently. It doesn't matter; the kid I was then couldn't do anything but run, escape. Just know you were the only regret I had, and still have to this day. Leaving Last Stand was easy. Leaving you was the hardest thing I've ever done.

You saved me, Sage. I know I've said it, but I don't think you realize I truly did mean it literally. Yes, you saved my sanity, you showed me how wrong they were, that my life wasn't right or normal. But I meant what I told you. That you really were the only reason I didn't take the easy way out, more than once. I thought about ending it so many times but never did because I couldn't do that to you. I knew you would blame yourself, even though it wouldn't have been your fault in any way. And now I know you saved me for good, when you went to your brother and fought for me. You were always fighting for me, even when I no longer had the strength to fight for myself.

I would never ask you to leave Last Stand because I know it's your heart, your blood, it's in your very soul. But I can't stay, Sage. I can't live with my past here. With just about everyone knowing, judging, not on who I am now but who I was then. I don't have any words for how much I wish I could. But wishing never got me anything. Wait, that's a lie. Because once, when I was little, I wished for one of those guardian angels they talked about. And that happened, the first day we met here at the creek. You were my angel, Sage. You always will be.

So I'll end like I started, since it's the beginning and the end anyway.

I love you.

Scott

Sage sat, staring at the lines of his bold, steady handwriting until they blurred from her tears. She saw the page shaking, realized her hands were trembling.

And in that moment she made the decision she'd never thought she would ever make.

Chapter Twenty-Two

SCOTT STARED OUT at the lines painted on the tarmac. How many airports in how many places had he been? He'd lost track. But one thing he was sure about. Even when he'd been boarding a transport heading into hell, to a place where death lurked in myriad corners in myriad ways, he'd never wanted to get on a plane less than he did right now.

"Going to or coming from?"

The voice from his right was quiet, but still startled him.

"What?" It was a measure of how off balance he was that he hadn't even noticed how close the other man was.

"Last time I paced an airport like you are, I was trying to get home in time to see my little boy born."

The man wore a kind expression and a smile. This, he thought. This was why he needed to be gone. Why he needed to be where nobody knew his past, where people didn't look at him as if they were remembering everything he'd ever done wrong, every bit of trouble he'd ever caused or gotten into. Where people like this total stranger would simply talk to him without that assessing look, as if they were waiting for him to do something terrible at any moment.

The agent at the counter made the call for the next group

to board the flight. He'd be in the next one, as apparently so would this amiable stranger.

"Did you make it?" he asked.

"I did." The warm smile widened. "And a better son never entered the world."

Scott managed a return smile, but he couldn't help wondering if his father had sounded that way when Pete was born. Probably. He'd surely sounded that way ever since. In his mind, there could never be a son as good as his firstborn. Which made any sacrifice, willing or not, worth it to him. And anyone who couldn't help worthless.

"At least," the man added, the smile becoming a grin, "until his brothers came along. Then it was a three-way tie."

And there it was, the difference.

All parents have favorites.

Not like yours! It's not normal, Scott. Not right. My father loved each one of us. In different ways, yes, but none of us ever doubted it. None of us ever felt we were less than the others to him.

You were lucky.

To have him? I know that. But just don't go thinking he's right, that...thing that sired you.

Sage had been so fierce that day. Her hands on her hips, eyes flashing as she stared him down, insisting what he was living with wasn't right or fair or to be tolerated quietly. But then Sage Highwater was and had always been a fighter. And so often she'd fought for him. She was amazing. She was—

Here.

Sage was here.

He gaped at her as she strode through the waiting area at the gate.

"Ah," the man beside him said. "The reason for the pacing? She looks like quite a woman."

"She...is."

"Take my advice, son. A woman who can put that look on your face is worth hanging on to," he said before discreetly moving away to give them room.

Scott stared at her. She was the Sage of a thousand memories. Tall, slender, long legs in blue jeans, and scarred boots that declared she was no show cowgirl but a real one, the long-sleeved pullover of some silky material the color of her eyes. It clung to her in a way that made his fingers curl. She had a backpack over one shoulder and a duffel in the other hand, and she was covering the floor between them quickly with those long-legged strides.

She came to a halt in front of him. He had to fight to find any words at all. "I...what are you doing here?"

"Looking for you, genius." *Uh-oh.* He knew that tone. She was fired up and full of sass.

"But you can't get to the gate without—"

"Buying a ticket." She waved her phone at him, and a boarding pass showed on the screen.

She'd bought an airplane ticket just to get through to here to talk to him? "Sage, what the hell?"

"I found your letter."

"Oh."

He'd labored over the thing for hours last night, knowing even as he did it that it was a futile effort. That moment in time, when he'd poured himself onto those pages ten years ago, was like lightning in a bottle, perhaps captured once but never again. So he'd started again, remembering Shane's advice, oft quoted by Sage. *Start where you stand.*

And when he'd tucked this one into that spot in the rocks—carefully protected in plastic this time, just in case—it had been painfully like saying goodbye all over again, not only to the girl who had saved him, but to his desperate seventeen-year-old self.

"You should have asked."

He tried to focus. "What?"

"You wrote that you never would, but you should have."

He stared at her. There was only one thing he'd written in that letter that fit what she was saying. "Ask you to leave Last Stand? That's crazy."

"How would you know? You know, Parrish, you take one hell of a lot for granted."

Belatedly, far too belatedly, the size of that backpack registered. And the duffel. "I—"

"If you're too stubborn to even give Last Stand a chance, then so be it. I'm not losing you again."

The agent at the counter made the boarding call for his row. He was suddenly aware that his mouth was dry, realized he was gaping at her, slack-jawed. "You can't leave."

"But you won't stay, not even long enough to figure out if anything's changed. So that only leaves one option."

"But the ranch, your horses—"

"Three brothers, remember? About time they were reminded running that ranch is no cakewalk."

"But your horse, the competition this summer, you've been working so hard—"

"Shane can ride him. Poke responds to his command presence."

"But your friend, Jessie, she needs—"

"Who do you think pushed me the hardest to go?"

"Sage—"

"And in case you missed the bottom line, it's that I love you, too."

Time seemed to slam to a halt. Those last words rang in his head like the bells of Father Nunes's church. Words he'd never expected to hear, not now, not after all this time, not after all that had happened. He gulped in air, only then aware he'd forgotten to breathe for a long, silent moment.

"You…"

"Love you. I. Love. Scott. Parrish. I have since I was sixteen, and I will until I'm a hundred and sixteen, if I have Minna Herdmann's luck. There, is that clear now?"

He couldn't wrap his mind around it. Sage Highwater, ready to leave Last Stand, to go with him?

"You can't," he whispered. "You can't leave. Last Stand is a part of you."

"You are a part of me."

She would actually do it. She was standing there, with a boarding pass, bags, ready to get on a plane and leave behind the place she'd always said she'd never leave. The place she'd always said was so deep in her bones she couldn't live anywhere else. Ready to go with him, when he didn't even know where he'd end up or what he'd do when he got there.

It was a bigger declaration of love than he'd made in that letter.

And a bigger declaration of faith.

He stood there staring at her, more rattled than he'd ever been, even under fire. After years of making or carrying out literal life-and-death decisions, he felt completely rudderless, at the mercy of a wind that seemed to be blowing only in one direction.

"Sage," he whispered.

He couldn't get out any more. He just looked at her. And then she dropped everything, crossed the space between them in a single stride, and threw her arms around him. He hugged her back. No, not hugged, held on. Held on as if for dear life, because suddenly that's what it was; he was holding the rest of his life in his arms.

After a moment he realized the sound he'd been hearing was clapping. Applause. They were being applauded by those filing onto the boarding ramp. No lewd comments, no judgments being passed, just a bunch of strangers who approved.

And Sage finally leaned back to look up at him intently. And he saw in her expression that she'd realized. "That's the difference, isn't it?" she said softly. "This is what would never happen in Last Stand."

He could only nod. Words were beyond him just now.

"Now," Sage said briskly, "you want to tell me why we're getting on a plane to Seattle?"

He blinked. "I just—" He stopped. His brow furrowed. "Wait. Are you saying you bought a ticket on this exact flight?"

"I did." She smiled, as if she were amused by his consternation. "It's a good thing my brother's who he is or he wouldn't have been able to get me here in time. He never, ever pulls rank with other agencies—like about speeding—for personal reasons, but he did it for me."

"But how did you even know that's where I was going? I only changed it this morning."

"Well, lo and behold, it turns out Ranger Buckley knows some people at this airline."

Scott blinked again. "And they just told him?"

"He's a Ranger," she said simply. "And he has quite the reputation, you know. He told them it was a family emergency. Which it was," she said, so pointedly he felt his stomach clench.

"You really called out your troops," he whispered past the knot in his throat. "Again."

The look she gave him then was so warm, so loving it made him shudder. "They're your troops now, too, you know. Unless you do something stupid like break my heart and send me away."

"I—" He had to stop to swallow. "I think I already broke it once."

"Yes, you did. But you had no choice, Scott. I know that." She reached up and cupped his face. He wanted nothing more than to press his cheek against her palm and stay there for the next millennium or so.

And Sage asked again, softly, "Why Seattle?"

He shrugged. "Never been."

"Nice try. You're going to look for Kane. For me." It

wasn't a question, so he didn't see any point in denying it, since it was true.

"I know there's not much chance, not in a city that big with no real clues except that he might have been headed there, but it was the only thing I could think of to do," he admitted.

"And I've been wanting to go since we found out Kane might be headed there. Would have, if my brothers hadn't talked me out of it." That eased his tension slightly. But then she went on, and an entirely new kind of tension spun up in him. "And sometime soon I hope I can show you what it means to me, that you would do it." Her voice went husky as she added in a whisper that nearly put him on his knees, "Very soon. I've waited nearly half my life for you, Scott Parrish. I'm tired of waiting."

There was no doubting her meaning, or the heat in her eyes, in her voice, and suddenly he wanted out of here, out of this airport, wanted to get someplace where he could do what he, too, had been waiting nearly half his life to do. Make love to the only woman who had ever fired his blood so fiercely he had never, ever forgotten what it felt like to touch her, be touched by her. They'd never even had sex and yet he'd felt more with her than anyone he'd ever been with.

The last call for boarding came over the speakers.

"We'd better go," she said.

He stared down into those amazing blue eyes. She held his gaze steadily. No wobbling, no regret. Because this was Sage Highwater, and when she made up her mind it was full speed ahead.

Chapter Twenty-Three

THERE COULD NOT, Sage thought, be a landscape in the country more different from Texas, except maybe Alaska. The tree-covered islands barely visible in the winter dark this far north, the brightly lit ferries crossing the water of Puget Sound, the thick clouds and the steady rain on the jet's windows as they turned and started to drop for the landing—all of it was like another world.

Was this what Kane had been looking for? A place so utterly different there could be no reminders?

And wasn't that what Scott was looking for, too? Someplace where no one knew him, where everyone he met was a stranger instead of someone who remembered the kid he'd been? Someone who knew only the surface story, and condemned him for not pulling together with his family in the face of potential tragedy? She smothered a sigh. Understanding didn't ease the ache in her heart at the thought of leaving Last Stand behind.

The longest conversation they'd had had been during the layover in Houston, when after some research on his phone Scott said, "We'll have to grab a shuttle to pick up the rental car a couple of miles from the airport. But we need to find a different place to stay."

"Different?"

"Where I would have stayed isn't good enough for you."

She'd reached over then and grabbed the phone from him, making him look at her. "You're talking to a woman who has more than once slept on a pile of straw in a barn."

The look he gave her then had her thinking all sorts of heated, pulse-hammering thoughts, of other things to do on that pile of straw. And the certainty surged in her anew; she might not want to leave Last Stand, but her future was with this man, no matter where he was.

That certainty had gotten her through the flight to Seattle, despite Scott's apparent need for silence. Beyond checking the weather—rainy and, by Texas standards, seriously cold—Scott had said little.

"You always this quiet on an airplane?" she'd finally asked.

He'd given her a steady look. "This is not the place for the conversation we need to have."

He'd slept, or at least dozed, the rest of the way. This had left her mind loose to wander, which was not necessarily a good thing. Because all she could seem to envision was a Scott in uniform, flying toward chaos and war. Had he slept then, too? Was his capacity for compartmentalizing that strong? Was that a necessity for that life?

When he'd awakened at the first instant the sound of the engines shifted as they began to descend, she thought she'd probably been right.

"Sorry," he muttered. "Haven't slept much for four

days."

Since he'd arrived in Last Stand. "Neither have I, frankly. I couldn't stop thinking about you."

She'd smiled at the first stunned, then sheepishly pleased expression that had crossed his face. And she smiled now, at the memory of it.

"Hang on to that thought, will you?" She snapped out of her reverie at his whispered words and heated up all over again at the rough edge in his voice. An instant later he took her arm and they left the rental car counter.

She'd thought herself ready but changed her mind at the first step outside into the rain and cold and dark. Her fairly lightweight jacket was not enough for her Texas born and bred blood. They started down the parking aisle the woman at the counter had indicated—a woman who had, Sage noticed, given Scott an appreciative look.

"We'll get the heat on as soon as we're in the car," he said, noticing. He always noticed.

"It feels as cold as it would have been if I'd come when I wanted to, when we first found out he was probably headed here," she muttered.

"Sean said that was around Christmas?" he asked as they reached the rather generic silver sedan.

She nodded. Then, giving him a sideways look, she asked, "You talked to Sean about it?"

He nodded. "He gave me the aged-up photo, Kane's vitals, as far as you know now, and the chain of what you've learned over the years." She blinked. "What, you thought I was going in cold? No idea what he even looked like now?"

"No, I just… Sean never said."

"I asked him not to." He lowered his gaze. "Because I didn't expect to find anything, and I didn't want you to get hoping again."

She didn't respond until they were in the car. He started it immediately and, as promised, cranked on the heat. It took a moment for the air to warm, but when it did she held her hands up to the vent before she finally said, "You didn't expect to find anything, but here you are."

"I told you, it was all I could think of to do. The only thing that…meant anything."

She gave him the only answer that told him what that meant to her. "I love you."

His head snapped around as if she'd shocked him, as if it were the first time she'd said it. *I would think that a man such as Scott, who suffered what he did at the hands of those who should have loved him, might need to hear it spoken. Perhaps repeatedly.*

"Sage," he whispered, as if that was all he could say.

And she knew now Elena had been exactly right. He would need to hear it often.

"I love you," she repeated and reached out to cup his face once more. The rest of what Elena had said came back to her. *He might not believe it until it is shown to him, proven.*

Well, she intended on proving it to him. Tonight.

"I…love you, too. I always have."

"So, second thing in the morning we start looking?" she said.

"It's a little late to start tonight," he agreed. "We—What

do you mean, second thing?"

"First thing is a continuation of what we start tonight." She said it casually, as if it were a given. Which to her, it was. She'd waited nearly half her life for this man, and she was tired, very tired of waiting.

She heard him swear under his breath, harsh and heartfelt. And then, after a moment and an audible sucking in of air, he said, "One room?"

"And a few more condoms," she said rather archly.

He blinked. "A few...more?"

"My brothers gave me what they had handy, but—"

"Your brothers?" He nearly yelped it, then gaped at her.

"Well, each of them thought he was the only one, of course." She gave him a look that matched her arch tone. "But I certainly hope three won't be enough."

"Not even close," he ground out.

And barked the tires as they headed out of the parking lot.

He'd made a reservation at a motel near the airport because he hadn't wanted to tackle finding his way around a big city strange to him at night. But there was no way he was going to have his first night with Sage be at some downscale place that he'd chosen for proximity, not style or amenities.

He took a shot that since it was Sunday evening, weekend visitors would have checked out, and landed a room at one of the more upscale places near downtown. With some help from his phone's map program they made it with only one missed turn. But when he pulled into the registration parking area, Sage was the one who yelped.

"This place? Are you crazy?"

He turned off the motor and looked at her. "I think I'm the one who should be asking you that."

"But this place is expensive! And it's—"

"Still not good enough for you."

"Scott, you don't have to—"

"I want to." He gave her a wry smile. "After tonight, we may rethink."

"If we don't choke on the bill first."

That was his Sage, ever practical. But he didn't want practical tonight. He reached out and took her hands in his. "Let me do this, Sage. For the ten years we lost."

For a moment she just looked at him. Then, softly, she said, "We didn't lose them, they were taken from us. But all right. Tonight."

Sage looked around the room. It was lovely, large, done in colors that she guessed would reflect the outdoors on a sunny day, rich greens and deep blues. There was a sitting area with a sofa and a flat screen, a minibar that wasn't really mini at all, a desk, and a small table with two chairs upholstered in a blend of the two colors that set the tone.

And the bed. Of course. Pristine. Immaculate. Just like the room. As if no one had ever set foot here before.

She felt an inward twinge; she would have preferred their first time be at home—

But it wasn't home anymore. She stifled the qualm.

She'd made the decision; it was done. Her home was with him, wherever he might be.

"We don't have to do this."

She snapped out of her thoughts and looked at him. He was watching her, with a steady calm belied only by the tight set of his jaw. He meant it, she realized. If she called a halt it would end. Silly, noble guy would probably sleep on the couch.

She turned to face him.

Sage had always thought him beautiful then, with green eyes vivid beneath the shaggy hair, even with the almost gaunt look and haunted expression he'd had at seventeen. But now, when he was strong, powerful, and carried a quiet confidence and self-possession he was…she couldn't think of any words strong enough. Could only think of one analogy.

It must have shown in her face, because he gave a low groan before saying, "Damn, Sage, whatever you just thought…"

"You don't want to know."

He crossed the six feet between them in two long strides, and again she thought of power, and grace. He took her hands and his fingers tightened around hers. "The hell I don't."

She felt her cheeks heat slightly. "You don't," she repeated. "You won't get it."

"Try me."

Oh, I want to. Every bit of you.

But he kept looking at her, demanding without words, without pressure, but with a quiet patience he'd never had before. And she realized suddenly that if she tried to outlast him she would lose; the man was trained to wait for hours, even days if he had to, to take out a target.

She gave in. And if he didn't understand, if he was insulted, maybe it was best she find that out now.

"I was thinking you're like Poke."

He blinked. Drew back slightly. "Your horse?" He looked startled, but not offended.

She nodded. "You're strong, powerful, and you have the same quiet, calm air now. But just like Poke, I know that could explode into stunning, flawless action in an instant."

She could have sworn she saw a faint flush in his cheeks, just as she had felt a moment ago. And it was a moment before she saw him swallow, then speak.

"Why did you think I wouldn't get...what a compliment that is?"

"A lot of people wouldn't appreciate being compared to a horse."

"Then they don't know how you feel about horses. That horse in particular."

You should have known. This is Scott, of course he understood. She smiled at him. "You mean that they're the most beautiful, noble creatures on the planet? Yes, that's how I feel. And Highwater's Hot Poco is the most magnificent one I've ever seen. Hence the comparison."

"Sage—"

"And if you don't make love to me right now I am going to go Texas-sized crazy."

"Well, now," he said, with the biggest Texas drawl she'd ever heard from him, "we can't have that."

And then, at last, God at last, he kissed her.

Chapter Twenty-Four

THE MOMENT SCOTT felt her mouth under his, all thoughts of a slow, gentle taking were blasted out of his mind. Still, he tried to ease back; this was Sage, whom he owed so much. Sage, his first love.

Sage, in truth his only love.

"Don't even think about going slow, Parrish," she said against his lips, as if she'd felt him shift, or as if, more likely, she could read his mind.

He broke then, as ten years of waiting breached the dam. His body surged to readiness so fast it took his breath away. He gave up on finesse as he pulled at that silky blue shirt, practically yanked it over her head. She didn't protest, in fact was tugging at his shirt, had it unbuttoned and pushed off his shoulders; he'd barely noticed so desperate was he to have her skin against his.

She had on a bra almost the same color as the shirt, blue and lacy. He thought he might appreciate the sight of her in it some other time; right now he wanted it gone. Again as if she'd read his mind—or more intoxicatingly wanted it herself—she reached back and unhooked it. He felt a split second of gratitude, because he wasn't sure he could have done it, the way his hands were shaking. And then the fabric fell away and he could barely breathe.

His hands slipped up her slender rib cage, and he swallowed tightly. Sage was slender and fit and strong, but her breasts were soft and full and rounded into his palms as if made for him. She arched her back, pressing herself against his hands. He brushed his thumbs over nipples that were already taut, and she sucked in an audible breath, then let it out as a low moan when he increased the pressure.

She leaned forward and pressed a hot, demanding kiss to the center of his chest. Then her hands slid down his belly and every muscle he had knotted in fierce anticipation. She tugged at the top button of his jeans, her fingers brushing over his erection. He nearly jumped at the jolt just that gave him, and she paused.

"Scott?"

"I've waited for this for so damned long," he muttered as he kissed her again. And again.

He wasn't even sure how they shed the rest of their clothes. How he got the condom on. It didn't matter, only having Sage naked in his arms mattered. They went down to the bed in a tumble, and he couldn't touch enough, taste enough. Only the fact that she was doing the same kept him from trying, futile though he knew it would be to rein it in. He was past the point, long past the point of any kind of control. And he took every bit of his fierce, strong Sage's response, the way she was touching him, kissing him, as if she'd felt every second of those ten years as strongly, as achingly as he had, as fuel to the fire they'd lit between them.

"Now," she said, her voice something he'd only heard in his dreams, low, husky, urgent.

It seemed only right that this be as basic, as elemental as it could get. He slid between her thighs, reached to stroke her. She was hot, wet, slick, and this proof she was as ready as he was was the final straw.

Don't even think about going slow, Parrish...

At the first sweet clasp of her flesh around his swollen cock he couldn't think at all, and he drove home in one slamming thrust. She was tight, impossibly so, and he shuddered.

She cried out his name, and for an instant he froze. But then she was repeating, "Yes, yes, yes," and he had to move. She arched up to meet his every thrust, her fingers digging into his back.

They slammed together until it was all he could do to hang on, to hold back. Just when he knew he couldn't last a second longer Sage cried out his name again, this time in a tone of wonder and awe as her body clenched fiercely around him, so fiercely he gave up even trying to wait and poured ten years of longing and love into her.

NOW THAT SHE could breathe again, now that the first ferocious need was sated—for now, for she wasn't anywhere near having had enough of him—Sage took advantage of the moment to prop herself up on one elbow and greedily study the man beside her.

It had been more than she'd ever imagined it could be, certainly more than she'd ever experienced. Hotter, more intense, more wonderful than even all her heated teenage dreams. Because he was more.

"I was wrong," she said softly.

His eyes, which had been closed as his breathing gradually slowed, flickered open. "Should I mark the calendar?"

She couldn't help grinning. She quite liked this new, carefree, even smartass Scott. "Oh, no need. This night will be engraved in my memory in neon."

"Can you engrave with neon?"

She gave him a playful swat on the shoulder. That strong, powerful shoulder at the top of arms that had flexed so beautifully as he moved over her, drove into her.

"I meant I thought I knew what…this would be like. With you. I grossly underestimated."

He smiled then. "So did I. And my estimates were pretty damned high."

She snuggled up close to him, stroking her hand from his chest to his ridged abdomen, savoring the way he shivered under her touch. She lingered over the gouge of rough, scarred flesh that ran along the lower right side of his ribs. He went still.

"What was it?"

"IED. Piece of shrapnel."

She only nodded. She'd had a chance to truly see him now, as he lay in what she called in her mind naked glory, without even the slightest laugh, because it was the only description that fit. She slowly leaned down and pressed her lips to the scar.

"Why did you do that?" he asked, sounding puzzled. Or as if he thought the puckered flesh was something she'd want to avoid.

She countered with her own question. "What does it mean to you?"

His brow furrowed. "An unwanted souvenir."

"I think it should mean you stared death down and won."

He looked startled, then lowered his gaze. But he looked pleased, albeit shyly. "It means that, too."

"And after you've done that, anything less is just that. Less."

His gaze shot back to her face. "And you say your brother the chief is the wise one."

"He is. And he did contribute a condom, after all."

She savored his rather sheepish grin. "Do I have to thank him?"

"Only when you feel up to it," she teased.

"Speaking of feeling up to it," he began.

"Oh, I noticed," she said with a delighted smile; she had always loved the boy she'd known, but she was becoming quite besotted with this confident, laughing Scott. The man she'd always known he could become, everything she'd known he could be, was here now.

She reached downward, closed her fingers around already taut flesh. He groaned, closing his eyes for a moment. She stroked him, base to tip, and savored the way his narrow hips lifted. She stroked a little harder, faster.

"Hey, cowgirl?"

She looked up at his face at the way the words seemed to have come from behind gritted teeth. Had she hurt him? "What?"

Then his eyes, those impossible green eyes opened. And she'd never had a man look at her the way he did then.

"Ride me," he said, his voice taut and hoarse.

A shiver of anticipation went through her.

And she did.

Chapter Twenty-Five

THIS PLACE HAD been, Sage thought, worth every penny. Although it was far from the pristine place they'd entered. She had grinned when, in the morning, she had looked around at the tossed pillows and tangled sheets.

And she would never think of Seattle as cold and gloomy again. Because it would forever be the place, not where her dream came true, but where reality had so far exceeded her dreams that she had no words to describe it.

And now, as they got into the car again, she didn't even mind the new soreness of her body, in fact she savored it as proof it had not been a dream, it had been real. Scott was finally hers in that most intimate way.

She wasn't sure she'd say it was worth the ten-year wait.

She was sure the ten years didn't matter anymore.

They easily found the Seattle Center where the iconic Space Needle stood, remnant of a World's Fair over a half century ago. A parking space, even on a Monday morning—well, still morning for a few minutes anyway Sage thought with a smile at how most of that morning had been spent—was something else again. They ended up over near what was labeled Memorial Stadium, a stone-looking edifice that Scott said seemed practically Roman next to the soaring metal of the wasp-waisted tower. She had no description for the colored blobs of random shapes that constituted the museum they walked past.

"Used to be a rock and roll history museum," Scott said, looking at the brochure they'd picked up in the hotel. "Now it's pop culture, too."

"Music?" She looked at it with more interest now.

"Yeah. Think he might have gone in, if he was here?"

She looked at the proximity to the towering structure they were here to see. "I think if he came to the Needle, he would have wanted to."

"As long as he wasn't too broke to buy a ticket," Scott said, scanning the posted rates. Sage winced. Scott immediately slipped an arm around her. "Sorry, I didn't mean—"

"I know. And I know it's probably true. I just hate thinking of my brother...struggling like that."

They went ahead with the plan, although the trip up the Needle was shorter than she'd thought it would be. Sage was no fan of what was apparently a recent renovation that included a glass floor at five hundred feet up. So they showed the photograph around and asked every employee they saw, got the negative response they'd expected, given they'd been told there were over a million visitors to the thing every year, and headed down.

"Probably seems silly to you," she said, silently thankful as her feet hit the ground again. "You've probably jumped out of airplanes fifty times higher."

"Nah," he said with a grin. "Maybe twenty times higher."

She gave him a slug in the arm, and he laughed. Not a sour or harsh laugh, but a pure, genuine one, with no undertones. Sage vowed she would hear more and more of that, enough so that when she thought of him laughing that would be the first memory that would come to mind, not the others.

They walked back toward the museum. It truly was a very…different sort of building.

"Melted crayons," Scott said.

"Dead sea monster," Sage countered.

She got the laugh again. "The former dripped over the latter," he agreed.

In fact, once she got inside—and finished staring up at the famous tornado-shaped tower of guitars—she found it fascinating, and was almost able to put out of her mind why they were here. They wandered the exhibits, or rather she did; Scott stopped to talk to every person they encountered with an ID tag on. She'd let him take the lead with it, for more reasons than she cared to think about right now.

There was a lot of stuff on old movies and television, and exhibits that made her grin at how cheesy some of the science fiction gear looked in person, away from the videos they'd appeared in. And small; she would have sworn that one movie villain had been huge.

Finally they reached the section called the Sound Lab, where there were small, individual booths where people could go in and pick up various instruments that were tethered to a sound system, pick a background track and then play along, take a lesson, or just plink. She stepped inside an empty one, although if there was a least musical Highwater, except for appreciating, she would be it. She ran a finger over the strings of the guitar. This would draw Kane. She knew it would. Music had been so important to him. As a child she'd always imagined he'd one day be a famous singer or songwriter.

Maybe he hadn't even known this place existed. But surely he would have once he got here? Then, how could he resist, if he could, as Scott had said, afford it? Not that it mattered. Who would remember him if he had? It seemed a lot of the people working here were volunteers, and the turnover was probably—

"Sage."

Something in his voice, some sense of urgency, made her step out of the small booth in a rush. He was standing a few feet away, next to a young woman wearing a name tag and an ID lanyard. His phone was in his hand, and she was looking at it. Looking at it and...

Nodding.

And for a moment, Sage forgot to breathe. She fought down the shock and moved toward them.

"I'm positive," the woman was saying when Sage got there. Her name, according to the tag, was Casey. "I remember because I'd just started volunteering here, and he was the first person I'd heard in here who could actually play. Most people just make noise, you know, before they figure out how to clean it up with the computers. He played. And he didn't need the computer's help to sound wonderful."

"You're sure it was him?" Scott asked.

The woman hesitated. Glanced from Scott to Sage. "He's not...like your runaway husband or anything, is he?" she asked, nodding again at the aged-up image Sean had given Scott. "He sounded like you. The accent I mean."

"No," Sage managed to get out, wondering what that had to do with anything. "Why?"

"I just...he was very nice-looking. I heard him singing. He had a beautiful voice." Sage went rigidly still at that. The woman went on, rather awkwardly, "If I didn't have a boyfriend, and it wasn't against the rules, I'd have flirted with him."

Sage realized Casey hadn't wanted to offend her, if indeed the man she'd wished she could flirt with was an errant husband. That made her like the woman. "He's my brother. Are you sure?"

She nodded a third time. "He wasn't someone I'd forget. Especially from my first week here."

"When was that?" Scott asked.

"Is he...in trouble?"

"Yes," Sage said rather fiercely, "because I'm going to clobber him when I find him, for making me worry all this time."

Casey smiled at that and said simply, "Last summer." Sage smothered a gasp. They had him down to less than a year ago? "He came in about five or six times when I was here." Her smile turned sad. "I teased him once that he could buy his own guitar with the money if he kept coming so often. He got very quiet. Said he had one, but he'd never,

ever hold it again."

Sage let out a sharp breath as an old pain jabbed at her. The memory of that day she'd gotten out his guitar, just to hold something that had been so important to him, slammed into her.

Then, suddenly, the woman's eyes widened.

"Wait…the song…it's you!"

Sage froze. Was utterly incapable of speech. But Scott was there, at her side, and he stepped in.

"What song?" he asked. The woman hesitated, and he added, "She's been looking for him for twelve years. Please."

"The song he used to sing when he was in here. About missing Texas, the hills, and…the flowers 'as blue as my sister's eyes.' Bluebonnets, he said when I asked him."

Sage still couldn't speak. She felt a shiver go through her, and an instant later Scott's arm was around her. She leaned into him, grateful for him for so many reasons now.

"Do you have any idea…where he might be?" Scott asked.

Casey sadly shook her head. "I just know that he came the last time around Halloween. I remember because all the kids visiting were in costumes." The sad expression deepened. "He actually thanked me, for being nice to him. And gave me the cutest drawing he'd done, a sort of caricature of me." She hesitated, glanced around, then said in lower tones, "I confess, I let him use my pass a couple of times to get in. But he didn't like doing it, so he turned me down the next time I offered."

Again a shiver rippled through her. So he hadn't thrown

everything away. He still had the conscience their father had hammered into them all.

And he still did those drawings. Like the one hanging on her bedroom wall.

"Anyway, he came and found me that day, because we were so busy. To say goodbye. I asked where he was going, and he said he didn't know, just that he'd been here too long. I'm sorry, I wish I could tell you more." The sad smile came again. "I really liked him. And I felt for him. He seemed so…so sad."

Sage was still reeling as Scott led her gently to a bench near a water fountain as the volunteer went off to deal with a malfunctioning keyboard.

"He was here. Right here," she whispered.

"Less than four months ago," Scott said.

"He's still alive."

She felt Scott go still. "What?" he asked.

"I was always afraid, when we'd find some new clue, that it wouldn't matter because somewhere up ahead we'd learn he died."

He hugged her tighter, both arms now, exactly what she needed. "Don't, babe. Don't think that. He's made it twelve years. He's not going to die on you before we find him. And we will find him. I promise you that."

Through the shock and sudden disquiet she was feeling, Sage only belatedly realized the depth of commitment in his words and his voice. He meant it.

And he meant that *we.*

Chapter Twenty-Six

IT WAS, SCOTT had to admit, a beautiful part of the country. The evergreens the place was named for, the blue Puget Sound waters, the boats, the birds, even bald eagles aloft, it seemed pristine even though he knew no place was without its problems. He didn't know but guessed even this lovely city had its share.

Of course, he thought the further they got from the city the more beautiful it was. But that was likely because he thought the best view of any city was from a safe distance.

The discovery at the museum had had Sage so wound up that they'd kept going, hoping against hope they could somehow find something else about where Kane might have gone. He very much doubted the possibility but he understood; this was closer than they had ever been.

Sage had called home the moment she'd gotten past processing what Casey had told them, so maybe her brothers could stir something up, now that they had some more recent information. In the meantime they'd kept looking, but after four days spent on fruitless trekking around and showing the photograph to others, they'd finally had to admit they'd likely hit the jackpot that first day and there wasn't anything left to find, at least not in the only way they had.

After she'd called her brothers again with the rather glum report of no results, she told him Shane had said they'd done all they could in a city that size. And that he'd put out some feelers while Sean had called a contact he'd met at a seminar, a detective who worked in the area although not in the city. Now that they knew the aged-up photo was fairly accurate, her brother had said, they could put more emphasis on it.

Scott wasn't upset about being told to stand down. It was a chance to simply spend time with Sage, time he'd never thought he'd have. And she seemed content to simply be with him, agreeing to whatever he suggested in the way of looking around the area. He insisted they stay at the hotel despite her worry about what it cost; there was time enough for him to economize later. Or so he told himself; in truth, he just wanted the best he could give her. At this point he'd be happy to just stay in bed with her around the clock, but he supposed since they were here they should at least look around. Then again…

Early Friday morning—too early—a vaguely familiar, annoyingly cheerful tune jolted him out of a sated sleep. He was sleepily trying to place it when Sage moved, her silken skin sliding over him in the process, and making him think maybe it wasn't so annoying after all. But it was barely 6 a.m. And they'd had a very…busy night.

Sage grabbed up her phone from the nightstand and he realized that was the source of the tune.

"Jessie," she said, and there was an undertone of anxiety

in her voice as she answered. Scott tensed. A wave of guilt surged through him. Sage had left her best friend trying to cope with her broken leg, to be with him. True, she'd said Jessie had told her to go, but still... It was enough to make him roll out of the bed; he'd head for the bathroom, give her some privacy.

But he stopped at the alarmed sound of her voice. "What's wrong? Is it your leg? Did you hurt it again? Is it the horses? You don't have another mare foaling, do you?" He stood, frozen, until after listening for a moment Sage let out a relieved breath. She looked at him and held up a hand to indicate everything was okay. Breathing again, he headed for the bathroom.

When he came out, Sage wore one of the most bemused expressions he'd ever seen on her face.

"What is it?"

She burst out laughing. "She called me—*me*—for clothes advice."

"I...isn't that what girls do?"

"But this is Jessie. She's never cared about clothes except to ask what pair of her multiple pairs of boots go with something. And now she wants to know what dress to wear tonight because that guy she met at PT is coming to dinner for Valentine's Day."

She was grinning so widely he couldn't help smiling back. But then the sense of her words hit him.

Holy crap.

"I...it's Valentine's day," he said, sounding rather stunned even to himself. And feeling as if he'd managed to make a monumental mistake. Already. "Sage, I'm sorry, I didn't realize."

Sage just laughed. "It's been Valentine's Day to me for a week now."

He looked at her. She wasn't mad? Didn't all women get mad if you forgot this day of all days? "I...I'm not used to..." He sucked in a breath and tried again. "It just never mattered before."

She was on her feet in an instant, and closed the distance between them in two long, leggy strides. "And that is the best gift you could give me," she said, stretching up to give him a kiss. And he'd wondered if any man had ever been so lucky.

On the recommendation of a grandmotherly type they met in the lobby of the hotel, they took a ferry ride, sampled the famous local clam chowder served aboard, which lived up to the hype, then rode the ferry back again just to see the city skyline as they approached.

"The city's beautiful...from here," Sage said. "I'd have to live on the other side if we stayed here."

He wasn't surprised she echoed his feelings; neither of them was cut out for big-city living. But it was still a little jolt every time she said something like that *if we stayed here* so easily.

But every time he reminded himself that this was Sage, and once she made up her mind she didn't waste time on regrets or second-guessing.

And she chose you. Over everything else she loves, she chose you.

With those words burning in his mind, he took it very slowly with her that night. There was nothing of the hot, fast, fiery sex they'd had before in it, only slow, tender, loving attention. He traced every inch of her, putting to use everything he'd learned about what she liked, until she was gasping at him to end it. But he made her wait, bringing her to the edge and then backing off until she very politely told him she was going to commit mayhem if he made her wait any longer to have him inside her. Then he learned that he'd been teasing himself as much as her, because when the moment came he thought sure he'd permanently singed something with the power of his climax.

And when Sage snuggled up next to him afterward he thought he'd never been so at peace in his life. Nothing else seemed to matter as long as she was here. Nothing.

After the first Valentine's Day of his life that meant something, they had a Saturday he'd only ever dreamed of. Late in the morning Sage announced she was buying breakfast, and did so by calling room service and ordering up a spread the likes of which he'd never seen before. And when it arrived, filling the table the smiling woman in the hotel uniform wheeled in, Sage followed her back to the door and tipped her—generously, Scott was sure.

An hour and a half later, he was nearly groaning he was so full. Sage just smiled at him, then got up, walked back to the door again, and hung out the Do Not Disturb sign. When she turned back, she was giving him that look that sent a sizzle through him and made his toes curl.

"Now we need to work that off," she said, and let the

hotel robe slip away as she walked back to him. Just watching her move like that did it, and they spent the rest of the day and half the night exploring in great detail what had finally been kindled between them. And even after that, Sage woke him up at some unknown hour. And she was in no mood for slow and gentle, and by the time she finished trailing her mouth over every inch of him, giving several crucial inches special attention, neither was he.

When she was done with him, he felt completely scoured out. And this time he was asleep before he could have another thought.

The man ahead of him was running, fast. And no matter how much Scott pushed, tried to pick up speed, he was always behind. And no matter how hard he ran, he still felt cold.

Finally, with the last breath he had, he yelled at the running man to stop. He did stop, and then slowly turned around. And Scott saw the face from the photograph they'd been showing around, but it was oddly blurred, as if there were some kind of fog between them.

"Stop running," he gasped out, winded.

The man laughed. "You're telling *me to stop running?"*

Scott awoke with a jolt. He lay frozen for a moment, staring into darkness. The hotel. They were still at the hotel.

The chill of the dream began to fade, in large part because Sage was curled up against him, warm, soft, sweet. And memories of last night, of skipping dinner for room service again so they could get to bed sooner, of Sage's apparent insatiability for him, so fierce it had seared him to the core, chased the last, lingering threads of cold into nothingness.

Because he knew he would never be cold again, not as long as he had her by his side.

He closed his eyes, wanting nothing more than to hold her close and drift back into sleep. Without the dream this time, hopefully.

You're telling me to stop running?

Dream Kane's laughing words jabbed him awake again. They echoed in his head in a sort of sarcastic litany. His stomach started to churn. Because for the first time in ten years he felt like an utter coward.

Sage had come to him, ready to fly off into the unknown for him, ready to leave everything she knew and loved, her entire family, to abandon every plan and hope she'd ever had for her future, while he was running from a fight for the first time in his life. He couldn't even tolerate being in the same town as his parents? Hell, he couldn't even face the disapproval of a small town and the snark of a few old ladies?

Give Last Stand another chance.

Give Last Stand a chance to redeem itself, in your eyes.

You need to make your peace with Last Stand.

Her whole family had rallied to his side when he'd needed support. But he couldn't give the town they all loved one more chance?

And suddenly another memory was crowding in. Daryl Mabrey, one of the injured of his platoon, after the mission that had later made them hang that star on him. Scott had been in a hospital bed, groggy but coming out of it, when he'd heard the man in the next bed telling someone whose back was to him, "Hell, I wasn't worried. Parrish is the toughest son of a bitch I've ever known. I knew he'd never give up. He'd get me out alive or die trying."

The absurdity of the contrast, that mission under fire and having his miserable parents, as her brother had put it, chewing on him hit him hard. For a moment he couldn't breathe.

She stirred beside him. "Scott?"

He opened his mouth to tell her to go back to sleep. The words wouldn't come. She sat up. Flipped on the light on the bedside table. He blinked at the sudden flare of light. But then all he saw was Sage looking at him, the bluebonnets of her beloved Hill Country re-created in the color of her eyes. The eyes of her brother's song.

She stared at him, and he wondered what must be showing in his face. "What is it?"

"I should have said can't."

She blinked. "What?"

"In the letter I said I would never ask you to leave Last Stand. I should have said I can't."

"You didn't. I—"

He raised a hand to put a finger gently over her lips, those luscious lips he hoped to soon be kissing again until they were both out of their minds. It didn't seem to take long.

"I can't ask you to do this. And I won't. I don't ever want you to hate me for making you leave."

"I made the choice."

"And showed me what I was doing in the process. Running. Running from a fight like a coward. And brave, gutsy

Sage Highwater would never stay happy with a coward."

She went very still. "What are you saying?"

"That you being happy is the most important thing in the world to me. And there's only one way to make sure of that."

"Scott…"

He drew in a deep breath. Let it out slowly. And said it. "Let's go home."

Chapter Twenty-Seven

"DO YOU ACTUALLY own a vehicle?" Sage asked as he tossed their bags in the trunk of the new rental car, this one with Texas plates. Good thing they both traveled light and didn't have checked bags to worry about.

He gave her a sideways look. "Thinking you're hooking yourself to a guy who's that broke?"

There was nothing, absolutely nothing he could say that would get a rise out of her. She was too happy. "Wouldn't care if I was," she said airily. "I was just wondering if you'd need to go get it, or if there would be future car shopping, or if you'd be okay with one of the ranch trucks."

He straightened and turned to face her. "Is that...where we're going?"

She caught the hesitation in his voice. She reached out to cup his cheek again. She loved the way he closed his eyes when she did, as if he wanted to shut out everything else except the feel of her touch. She savored it for a moment before deciding it was time to snap him out of old habits.

"Unless you want to go to your parents' place," she said sweetly. His eyes snapped open and he gaped at her. She grinned at him. "Come on, Parrish. After all you've faced and stood up to in your life, this is nothing."

His expression shifted to a rueful smile. "Old habits die hard."

"As long as they die," she said cheerfully. "Come on. If we hurry, we can make it in time for the family dinner." She saw it register. "Yep. Right into the fire."

"Thanks," he said wryly.

"Can you handle it? My brothers, I mean?"

"I'll manage. Although I may wish I'd brought my sidearm."

"Nah, the house is a fire-free zone. Not that they won't give you a hard time, mind you."

"Can't wait," he said dryly.

She hesitated, then decided she had to say it. "Fair warning, though. Sunday dinner is kind of a commitment."

"It is?"

"It's assumed if a Highwater cares about somebody enough to bring them, it's serious. Are you serious?"

This time it was he who reached out to cup her cheek. And she suddenly knew her guess had been right, that was exactly why he closed his eyes. But she made herself keep hers open despite the tremendous temptation. Because she needed to see his face when he answered.

"Utterly, absolutely, completely, probably deliriously serious."

"In that case, you're looking at Monday morning."

He blinked. "What?"

"Sunday dinner is serious. Staying until Monday morning is a declaration of intent."

Something changed in his face, his eyes. She saw him realize the depth of that invitation in the way those green eyes went hot and intense. "Oh, I have intent all right." His voice was low and rough and sent a shiver of nearly unbearable anticipation through her. And suddenly Last Stand and the ranch seemed too far away. On another planet too far away.

"Maybe we should spend the night here," she said huskily. "Find a place right now."

He sucked in an audible breath. Muttered an oath under his breath that was so clearly heartfelt it gladdened her. But then, slowly, he shook his head. "I think there's a gauntlet I need to run first."

Something powerful jabbed at her, and it took her a moment to realize it was an incongruous combination of admiration and exasperation…and hunger. She let out an audible sigh, crossed her arms, and gave him an exaggerated glare. "You know, for the town bad boy, you're annoyingly honorable."

"Sorry for failing to uphold my reputation."

For an instant she thought she'd hit too close to home, but then she saw the faintest twitch at one corner of his mouth. That wonderful, luscious mouth she wanted to taste for hours. That mouth she wanted all over her, just as she wanted to trace every inch of him with hers. Again.

"A reputation you never deserved," she said softly. "Can we hurry this up? I have plans for later."

"Oh, I hope so," he breathed, and she noticed his right hand was curled into a fist, so tight his fingernails had to be digging into his palm.

This clear sign that he was as ready as she was sparked her to add, with all the promise she could manage in her voice, "And I'm guessing they're going to take all night."

She smiled at his barely stifled groan.

They worked their way out of the airport, Scott at the wheel. "Might as well get used to driving in Texas again," she teased.

"Always an adventure," he said. Then, at the next red light, he glanced at her. "I'm not broke, by the way. I never spent much, and stayed in base housing whenever I could."

"What about after? Where were you living when you came here?"

She half expected him to comment on the past tense, but he didn't. "I crashed with a couple of buddies who had a place." His mouth quirked. "I'm sure they'll be glad to have their couch back."

A few minutes later they were on the 290 headed west to Last Stand. Home. She was thinking about calling Jessie, both to let her know they were home and to see how her new romance with Asher Chapman was going when he spoke again.

"You really would have done it," he said. "You would have left Last Stand."

"If that's the way it had to be, yes."

After a moment he started to speak again. "I don't—"

"If you say you don't deserve it, I swear I will throw you in the nearest nest of rattlesnakes."

He shot her a sideways glance, and she saw humor glinting in those vivid green eyes before he looked back at the road and said mildly, "I was going to say I don't know where to start with your brothers."

She gave him a wide-eyed look. "Oh, don't worry about that. Believe me, they'll start it for you." He winced. "Maybe you should have taken me up on that idea about staying here and heading back tomorrow."

He drew in an audible breath. "Nope. I have...a declaration to make."

Her own breath caught. And again the paradox struck her that he, who had long ago been dismissed by most people as pure trouble, had more honor in his little finger than most of them would ever have.

HE HADN'T EXPECTED...EVERYONE to be there when they walked in. He supposed he should have, but family dinners weren't something he was used to. But the sight of everyone gave him a qualm, and he felt as if he were floundering into the unknown.

"Well, well." Slater, watching him thoughtfully.

"Change of plans?" Sean, a bit too innocently.

He set his jaw and looked at the chief. Who said nothing. Yet.

"Lighten up, all of you," Sage said warningly.

The chief's gaze flicked to his little sister, then back to Scott. "If he can't stand up to us, then he's not man enough for you."

The man had a point.

There was a silence in the room that felt...expectant. Scott had no experience with this, either, this kind of family dynamic. He did, however, know a lot about dealing with brothers in arms. And he met Sage's eldest brother's gaze levelly.

"Maybe I should remind you I was a sniper. A good one. You might want to think about that before you launch on me."

For an instant the silence held. And then Shane Highwater smiled. It quickly became a grin, and Scott heard laughter around the room and somebody, Slater he thought, saying, "Nicely done."

But he kept his eyes on the imposing figure of the police chief. "That mean you're not throwing me out?"

"I think," the man drawled wryly, "you're laboring under a misapprehension of who really runs things around here."

"And she," Sean said, stepping over to clap him on the shoulder, "has clearly already decided."

"Welcome to Sunday dinner," Lily said cheerfully.

Sean turned his head and let out a piercing whistle. Scott's brow furrowed, but the unspoken question was answered when he heard the sound of running feet, and Marcos burst into the room.

"I'm starved, is it time to—" The boy broke off the instant he spotted Scott. He ran over and looked up at him, clearly excited. "You're here! They said you were gone."

"We came back."

"I'm really glad." He nearly gaped at the boy, at the enthusiasm and genuine delight in his voice. "You wanna play a game with me 'n Sean after dinner?"

"I...sure."

With a wide grin the boy ran over to the table, where Sage and Sean were adding two place settings and chairs. Elena de la Cova walked over and laid a gentle hand on his arm. "They are a very good family, Scott," she whispered. "Enjoy the change."

He fought down a flush, the instinctive reaction to anyone knowing his past, that he'd been utterly rejected by his own family. It was an old childhood fear, that people would look at him and think, "I see why." But Elena had put it in a way that made it clear what her view was. The Highwaters were a good family, whereas his was...not.

She was on his side. He glanced around, saw Joey Douglas—when had she done the red streak in her hair thing?—grinning at him from where she stood beside Slater. Then he looked at the rest of them. And there was no denying what he saw there. Welcome.

They were all on his side.

Chapter Twenty-Eight

SCOTT WAS STILL processing, a little stunned at what he'd just experienced. The closest he'd ever come to this was at mess with a group of fellow Marines, when the easy camaraderie had made it a pleasant change from the silent meals he'd grown up with, before he'd been declared too rude to sit at the family table and banished to his room for meals. Which he'd quickly decided he preferred anyway.

And this dinner, although minus the rough language and occasional braggadocio, had the same feel as those times at tables at a base, or in an olive drab tent. The same sense of being part of a close-knit group. He supposed his wonder must have shown in his face because, as they were digging into a delicious pecan pie from Char-Pie, Sage leaned over and whispered, "This is the way it's supposed to be."

He was so bemused by all this that he hadn't really thought about what would come next. Sage had told him that each of her brothers had a separate wing of the house, set up like private apartments with kitchenettes and separate entrances, all part of her father's plan to keep the family under one roof, here on the ranch. Her domain, she'd told him, was the upstairs, which had a similar setup.

"So nobody has to see anybody if they don't want to," she'd said.

What she hadn't said was that the stairway to her domain was in plain sight from the living room. Which meant that every person here tonight would know if they went up together.

They all pitched in to clear the table, then the women clustered in a corner of the kitchen. Sage was laughing, apparently at something Elena had said. Scott never would have thought the elegant, self-possessed woman could have such a wry sense of humor. Then they were talking so quietly he couldn't hear anything, which made him a little nervous. Nervous enough that he excused himself to step outside.

He walked the short distance over to the corral next to the barn. A horse ambled over to see if he was of any interest. When he realized this was the famous Poke, he was grinning—no doubt sheepishly—before he even thought about it.

You're strong, powerful, and you have the same quiet, calm air now. But just like Poke, I know that could explode into stunning, flawless action in an instant.

And then he realized he was almost blushing. In front of a horse.

"Hope you're not insulted, buddy," he said quietly. The animal seemed to study him for a moment, then nickered softly. Scott took the chance and reached out to pat him on his sleek, golden neck.

He suddenly felt once more the sort of twitchiness that down range had always warned him they were being watched. He looked to his right, saw Shane a few feet away. He'd suggested Scott drop the "Chief" over the pie, but he wasn't sure he'd be able to manage that out loud anytime soon.

He turned to face him. Sage's big brother kept coming. Stopped, reached out to stroke the horse's nose. Then he looked at Scott.

"Glad you came back," he said.

"I know you didn't want her to leave," he began.

Shane shook his head. "That was her call. We didn't like it, but it was her decision."

"Thought she was making a mistake?"

Shane studied him for a silent moment. "I thought she might regret leaving Last Stand. But I knew she would never regret going to you."

Scott stared at this man who, he had finally had to admit, he respected more than anyone outside the Corps. Finally, because it was the only thing he could think of, he said, "I love her. More than I thought possible."

"I know. Which is why what I really meant was I'm glad *you* came back."

"I think you mean that."

"I do. Just don't ever hurt her," Shane added.

Scott made himself hold the man's gaze. "I never, ever meant to. Of all people, never her."

"I believe that. Or you wouldn't have been so accepted here tonight."

"One more thing," Scott said.

"What's that?" Shane asked, his tone casual.

"I'm staying until morning."

Shane went very still. Scott stared him down, knowing if he backed down now it would forever tarnish his place here. And then, slowly, Shane Highwater, the unwilling but indomitable patriarch of the Highwater clan, smiled.

"Well, then," he said. "Welcome home, Scott."

"JUST LIKE THAT?" Scott asked incredulously a week later, staring at the key ring in his hand.

"Problem?" Mike Fleming asked, sounding unconcerned.

"I just walk in off the street, with my reputation, and you give me a job and hand me the keys, without a second thought?"

"Oh, I had a second thought. About hiring a Marine, I mean. But I think I can forgive you for being a leatherneck. If you call me Mike."

Scott shifted his gaze to the older man's face. It took him a moment, but he recovered his equilibrium. "Then I can stomach working for a ground pounder. Mike."

Mike grinned at him. They shook hands. And Scott had a job. God help him, in Last Stand.

He was still shaking his head in wonder when he drove back into town for the coffee Shane had asked if he could pick up. He didn't mind, didn't feel like the newbie errand boy, because the feeling of being so welcome at the Highwater ranch hadn't worn off. He was thinking just maybe it never would, and that was a quite an adjustment.

And it wasn't just Sage, although she was the most amazing thing that had ever happened to him, it was everyone. They were all treating him as if he were one of them by blood, and when Sage had softly whispered last night, "So how does it feel to have a real family?" his throat had closed up on him and he hadn't been able to get out a single word.

But Sage had understood. Because Sage always understood.

He spotted Father Nunes and an empty parking spot at the same moment, so pulled in. The man smiled and waved when he saw him, and waited while Scott got out of the ranch truck he was borrowing until he decided what to do about wheels.

"Glad to see you back," the man said.

"It's for good," Scott said.

"Room for you now that your parents are leaving?"

Scott blinked. "What?"

"You didn't know?"

Scott had the thought that not so long ago his answer would have been a bitter "How would I?" But now he only smiled at the priest. "You did?"

Father Nunes laughed as if he understood all the subtext of Scott's reaction. And perhaps he did. "I hear things. The real estate agent they listed their home with is in my parish."

"Oh." So they were really leaving. He wouldn't have to live wondering—wondering, but not really caring—if he'd run into them every time he was in town.

"You'd already decided to stay?"

Scott nodded. "They don't run me anymore."

The man's smile widened. "Good for you."

Scott started to speak, then hesitated. He had no idea what the etiquette was for this, but he felt he owed the man something. "You helped with that. Thank you."

"My job," Father Nunes said.

"Even though I'm not one of yours?"

"Counsel where it's needed," he answered simply.

Scott was still smiling at that as he approached the statue of Asa Fuhrmann on the corner in front of the library. Then his phone announced an incoming text. He pulled it out and was startled to see it was from Robbie. But he was even more startled when he read the four short words.

Did you mean it?

There was only one thing he could think of that that could reference. That moment after the funeral, when he'd told his brother if he ever wanted to get out of the cage they had him in, to come to him and they'd figure something out. Could his little brother have found his spine? Was he going to stand up to them at last, and not go with them wherever they were going?

He couldn't text back fast enough.

I did.

Can we talk about it?

Name the time and place.

Moments later they had a meeting set for tomorrow afternoon, out at the range. He hoped Mike's goodwill would extend to him taking a break for this on his first day. He had a feeling he would understand, and he'd work later to make up for it.

Maybe he'd even teach the kid to shoot. He grinned inwardly at the thought of an armed Robbie facing down the old man and telling him to get lost.

He started out again toward Java Time, the coffee shop. Thought about how different everything seemed. Even Last Stand felt different now. Some people smiled at him, a few even waved a greeting. Had that happened before and he just hadn't seen it, blinded by memories?

"Thank you for your service," the man at the cash register said as he handed him the receipt and the bag.

This was the fifth time he'd heard it this morning, and the third time he'd had no clue how the person even knew who he was. It wasn't like any of these people had been at the funeral, where Sage had made such a point of blurting out his record to anyone who'd listen.

Twice he'd at least recognized the person saying it. Once it had been the father of one of his classmates, who spoke quite respectfully, once it had been the sister of one, who had given him a charming look followed by a flattering smile. Both of which he was certain he never would have gotten ten years ago.

He'd been reduced to simply saying thank you because he was so stunned. He'd had this happen elsewhere, usually when he was in uniform or at some function where his service was clear.

He'd never, ever expected to encounter it on the streets of Last Stand.

"It's nice," the man, whose name tag said he was Fritz, added, "to have a hometown hero back home."

He blinked. "I…thank you, but I'm not—"

He broke off when the guy grinned widely. "Funny, that's exactly what *The Defender* article said you'd say."

Damn. Lily's profile. He'd forgotten about that. She'd told him last week it was coming out today, but he'd forgotten. And she had refused to let him read it ahead of time. He was beginning to see why.

"You didn't know?" Fritz asked, and Scott gathered his expression had mirrored his consternation.

"I knew about it," he muttered, "but I forgot it was out today."

The man reached over to the stack of the town newspaper that sat on the counter next to the impulse-buy rack. He picked one up and handed it to Scott.

"On the house," Fritz said. "Least I can do."

Scott took it. He didn't want the freebie, but he figured it would seem ungracious if he quibbled about it. When he got back to the ranch pickup he'd driven into town—encountering two more citizens effusively thanking him on the way—he finally opened the thing up. He blinked when he saw the headline at the bottom right corner of, of all places, the front page.

By the time he was done he was grateful he was alone in the car, because he was sure he was damned near blushing.

She made me sound like Carlos freaking Hathcock.

When he got back to the ranch—sparing a moment to acknowledge once more that after merely a week it felt more like a home to him than his parents' house ever had—he belted into the house in a rush.

"I need to talk to you."

"I need to talk to you."

He and Lily said it simultaneously, the moment he came into the kitchen where she and Shane were sitting with mugs of coffee.

Shane had, Sage had told him, actually begun to take the occasional weekend day off, although he was ever and always on call, just as Sean was. She'd shown him the cell tower installed on the ranch to be certain those calls could get through, which explained why he'd never had a problem getting a signal, even when they were out riding. Which he was getting better at, although he knew he'd never be at her level, not when she'd practically been born in the saddle. And that thought always reminded him of the childhood picture she'd shown him once, of her and her best friend, Jessie, at about age five, both mounted on horses that were probably average-sized but seemed huge in comparison to the little girls astride them, holding hands as they watched some activity in the corral in front of them.

He reeled his thoughts back in as Shane—and it was still hard not to call him Chief, or sir—nodded at him and said, "Ladies first is customary, I believe."

Lily gave him a loving smile. The kind of smile Scott had always envied—until this week, when Sage had so often looked at him the same way. Then the redhead looked back at him.

"I saw Judge Morales yesterday," she said.

Scott blinked. Warily he said, "Oh?"

"He wants a copy of that official photo of you. I told

him I'd see he got it."

He stared at her. "Why does he want that?"

"Surely you noticed the wall when you were in his chambers? With photographs of success stories, of people he admires and respects?" She smiled and glanced at Shane, a resident on that wall, for an instant before she looked back at him. "He calls it his wall of honor."

"I noticed, but what's that got to do with—" He broke off and drew back, startled at the thought that had occurred to him. Him? On that wall?

"Still not used to it, are you?" Shane said quietly.

"Time to shed that old skin, Scott," Lily said, her voice soft.

"Yeah, well," he muttered, "you kind of ripped it off with that profile you wrote."

Shane grinned at him then. "Interesting trip to town, was it?"

He realized belatedly he'd been set up when Shane had asked him if he could make that stop in town for coffee, which they clearly hadn't needed at all. But he focused on Lily. "You made me sound like…like…"

"Just what you are. A hero."

"Hardly."

"Tell me one fact I got wrong."

"You got the facts fine, but the rest… There are a thousand guys who've done what I did, and a lot who did a hell of a lot more."

"So it's my interpretation of the facts you're arguing?"

"I'm not arguing, it's just there are people who deserve

all that…that praise more than I do."

"Sticking to Last Stand narrows that down a bit, thankfully. But," Lily said cheerily, "I'll get to them all eventually."

Before he could think of a thing to say he felt that now familiar tickle at the back of his neck. He looked around and she was there, leaning one shoulder against the doorjamb, long legs—God, those legs, wrapped around him last night—crossed at the ankles, smiling at the two at the table.

"You know," she said in a voice as warm as the smile, "I really love this family of mine."

"Back at you," Lily said with a wink, drawing Scott's gaze back to the table, where Shane just smiled, nodding slowly in obvious satisfaction.

Scott met the man's gaze, noticed as always the difference of eyes a darker shade of blue than Sage's bluebonnet, and said quietly, "You've built an amazing family. I know it was you who held them together."

Shane lifted a brow at him. "It feels almost complete now."

Even with all the platitudes he'd heard today, Scott thought he'd never been paid a higher compliment. And he said something he'd often thought but never voiced, even to Sage. "I always had you in the back of my mind as the kind of man I wanted to be."

He had the pleasure of seeing the usually imperturbable Shane Highwater totally disconcerted. In the next instant Sage was beside him, her hand on his arm.

"You'll have to excuse us," she said, her voice sounding odd. And when he looked at her he saw her eyes gleaming with moisture, which startled him.

"Sage?"

"I love you." Her voice was so tight it almost hurt to hear. Hurt in a beautiful, wonderful way. And all he could do was pull her into his arms.

"Hold off on that until you get upstairs, okay?" Lily suggested, but she was grinning.

They did hold off until they got upstairs to her quarters. But barely.

"YOU'RE SMILING," SAGE observed lazily. She lay with one leg thrown over his, her body pressed against his side, his arm around her, savoring the feel of his skin, of his heat. She was feeling deliciously sated, for the moment. But she knew the hunger was only temporarily abated. That's all it ever was, with him.

Scott grinned up at her. "And why not? It's the middle of the afternoon and I just got ridden to a standstill by the best cowgirl in Texas."

"You'll recover," she teased.

"I will," he agreed. "And fast. We've got ten years stored up."

She leaned down and kissed him. "And when I say thank you for your service, remember I mean something entirely different."

He burst out laughing, and Sage knew she would never, ever tire of hearing that sound. She propped herself up on her elbow. "You don't regret coming back?" His gaze slid over their entwined naked bodies. "Besides that, I mean," she said with a grin.

"No," he answered. "No regrets. But…"

When he looked away she felt a twinge of unease. "What, Scott?"

"I meant what I said to Shane," he said, still not looking at her. "About the family he built."

"I know you did. And he earned every word of it."

"Yes."

He still wasn't looking at her. And that unease grew a sharper edge. "Out with it," she demanded.

"I love you, Sage. More than I have words for. But…"

Sage's heart slammed in her chest. "I don't like the sound of that 'but.'"

Finally he looked at her again. "You're going to want to have kids to add to that family."

She frowned. "Someday, yes." She tried a smile. "I'd like a boy with your eyes. Or a girl with them, so she can mow down every guy she meets."

He smiled back, but it didn't last and it was achingly sad while it did. "I can't do that, Sage."

She drew back sharply. It took her a moment to choose her words. "Do you mean that literally? Was there an…injury you didn't tell me about? Because, sure as Texas, everything seems to be functioning way beyond fine."

"No! No, it's not that it's just…"

His voice trailed away, and his expression told her. "You're afraid to have kids. Afraid you'll be like your father."

"I can't promise I won't be," he said harshly, proving her guess right.

"You don't need to promise," she said, "because I can. You are absolutely nothing like him. Nothing, down to the bone, Scott. How you are with Marcos proves that, not that I needed proof of something I know with utter certainty."

His gaze narrowed. "Nobody can—"

"I can," she said blithely. "But if you need insurance, you've got it. We'll live here on the ranch, and if you show the slightest, tiniest veering toward being like that nasty piece of work, my brothers will kick your ass. And then I'll toss you into that nest of rattlesnakes."

He blinked.

"And," she went on, "just think about those lucky kids, having what you never had. A big, loving family who thinks the world revolves around them. *All* of them." She saw it register, pressed on. "I haven't forgotten who you became, what you did in that uniform. You're a protector, like Shane. And I think those who protect sometimes have to go through hell to make sure they recognize it so they can keep it away from us."

He looked as if he'd seen a glimmer of light appear on a dark horizon. "Sage…"

"What did you just think?" she asked, because suddenly it was crucial that she know.

"That…I feel like I did when I'd hear the choppers for exfil. That safety was within reach, that…we were going to make it."

"We," she said with emphasis, "are going to make it,

Scott Parrish."

And she saw a different kind of smile spread across his face, one not haunted by his past or what had been done to him. Joy blossomed in her, and she had the very unexpected thought that she might want to get started on that kid thing sooner than she'd planned.

"Yeah. Yeah, we are." And he said it in the tone of a vow.

She put on an exaggerated scowl. "Only one problem."

"What?"

She couldn't hold the expression and broke into a grin. "More 'S' names for those kids."

He looked startled, then laughed. And she felt full almost to bursting with joy and love and some things she couldn't even name. But after a moment he gave her a serious, steady look. "Then we'll have to start a new trend with those kids."

"A new one?"

"Maybe Kate. Or Kyle," he said, still looking at her steadily.

Kate. Kyle. *K*'s. Kane.

She did burst then, the joy and love overflowing. She couldn't be even these inches away from him any longer, and she dropped down to drape herself over him, savoring every inch of sleek skin and muscle beneath. And a certain several inches immediately responded, declaring that recovery they'd talked about. She reached for him, stroked him, loving the way his hips moved and he sucked in his breath. She leaned down and pressed her lips to the scar on his side, that badge of honor that was worth more to her than any of the kind with ribbons attached.

"Welcome home, Scott," she whispered against his chest.

"You think you could say that while riding again?" he asked hopefully.

Sage laughed, and proceeded to do just that.

The End

If you enjoyed this book, please leave a review at your favorite online retailer! Even if it's just a sentence or two it makes all the difference.

Thanks for reading *Lone Star Reunion* by Justine Davis!

Discover your next romance at TulePublishing.com.

If you enjoyed *Lone Star Reunion,* you'll love the other books in....

The Texas Justice series

Book 1: *Lone Star Lawman*

Book 2: *Lone Star Nights*

Book 3: *A Lone Star Christmas*

Book 4: *Lone Star Reunion*

Book 5: *Coming June 2020!*

Available now at your favorite online retailer!

More books by Justine Davis

The Whiskey River series

Book 1: *Whiskey River Rescue*

Book 2: *Whiskey River Runaway*

Book 3: *Whiskey River Rockstar*

Available now at your favorite online retailer!

About the Author

Author of more than 70 books, (she sold her first ten in less than two years) Justine Davis is a five time winner of the coveted RWA RITA Award, including for being inducted into the RWA Hall of Fame. A fifteen time nominee for RT Book Review awards, she has won four times, received three of their lifetime achievement awards, and had four titles on the magazine's 200 Best of all Time list. Her books have appeared on national best seller lists, including USA Today. She has been featured on CNN, taught at several national and international conferences, and at the UCLA writer's program.

After years of working in law enforcement, and more years doing both, Justine now writes full time. She lives near beautiful Puget Sound in Washington State, peacefully coexisting with deer, bears, a pair of bald eagles, a tailless raccoon, and her beloved '67 Corvette roadster. When she's not writing, taking photographs, or driving said roadster (and yes, it goes very fast) she tends to her knitting. Literally.

Visit Justine at her website JustineDavis.com

Thank you for reading

Lone Star Reunion

If you enjoyed this book, you can find more from all our great authors at TulePublishing.com, or from your favorite online retailer.

Made in the USA
Middletown, DE
06 August 2023